Maze Of Secrets

"Do you think Clarice Carmichael might have killed her husband?" Irmajean Lloyd watched as her husband Glenn lowered the morning newspaper and fixed her with a where-did-that-come-from look.

"Does it matter after all this time? It's been what— seventy plus years?"

"Any bit of human interest matters. It definitely would add spice to the house tours at Rosewood. Heaven knows we need all the help we can get raising money to keep the estate up and running." A volunteer gardener and a member of the board of directors at historic Rosewood, she was learning the hard way what it took to keep such a place operating. "People pay their five dollars for a tour of the house and garden, and they want to hear interesting stories about the people who lived there.

What They Are Saying About

Maze Of Secrets

"Move over Miss Marple and Jessica Fletcher. Irmajean Lloyd is here."

—Suzanne Hurley

"Maze of Secrets is a mystery that keeps you turning the pages to uncover the secrets and solve this brilliantly-written whodunit."

—Linda Rettstatt

Maze Of Secrets

by

Norma Seely

A Wings ePress, Inc.

Cozy Mystery Novel

Wings ePress, Inc.

Edited by: Sara V. Olds
Copy Edited by: Christie Kraemer
Senior Editor: Lorraine Stephens
Executive Editor: Lorraine Stephens
Cover Artist: Pat Evans

All rights reserved

Wings ePress Books
http://www.wings-press.com

Copyright © 2008 by Norma Seely
ISBN 978-1-59705-691-5

Published In the United States Of America

September 2008

Wings ePress Inc.
403 Wallace Court
Richmond, KY 40475

One

"Do you think Clarice Carmichael might have killed her husband?" Irmajean Lloyd watched as her husband Glenn lowered the morning newspaper and fixed her with a where-did-that-come-from look.

"Does it matter after all this time? It's been what—seventy plus years?"

"Any bit of human interest matters. It definitely would add spice to the house tours at Rosewood. Heaven knows we need all the help we can get raising money to keep the estate up and running." A volunteer gardener and a member of the board of directors at historic Rosewood, she was learning the hard way what it took to keep such a place operating. "People pay their five dollars for a tour of the house and garden, and they want to hear interesting stories about the people who lived there. Not just that the floors are oak, the fireplace tiles imported from Italy... Besides, people ask questions and we don't have many answers. Which makes it look like we haven't done our homework."

"I don't see how you can be expected to know every last detail."

Irmajean dipped her tea bag up and down in her cup and then wrapped it around her spoon, squeezing every last bit of flavor from it.

"You'd be surprised what people expect us to know. And Priscilla doesn't want to disappoint anyone." She felt quite responsible for Priscilla, a friend of their daughter Gemma, since she'd been instrumental in hiring the young woman to be director of historic Rosewood Estate-the 1894 Queen Anne style mansion and five-acre garden bequeathed to the local historical society by the late Chalmers Carmichael. "Clarice was a bit of an enigma and visitors want to know why she became almost a recluse. For that matter, *I'd* like to know."

"And you think it would bring in more money if Clarice turned out to be a murderer?"

Irmajean again wrapped the string around her tea bag, strangling it. "Priscilla is looking for ways to draw more visitors to the property. A juicy mystery would be just the ticket."

Glenn Lloyd folded his newspaper with a sigh and focused his attention on the woman he'd been married to for thirty-five years. "If it's mystery you want, it seems to me you've already got it in not having all the answers. Let people speculate on what might have happened."

Irmajean shook her short brown curls and pursed her lips. "No, we need more than that. The number of visitors is down and other than two June weddings booked for the Rose Garden, we have absolutely nothing happening."

"And you think a murder would change all that?" His tone was skeptical.

"Of course! People may shudder at the thought, but they do like to hear the grisly details. Look how they flock to supposedly haunted houses. Besides, whatever happened—if indeed a crime was committed—it was so long ago it can't affect anyone alive today. Or anyone that we know of. Clarice's only child, Chalmers, died without heirs." She poked at her now cold poached egg.

Glenn looked at his wife and then his newspaper with longing. "What gave you the idea Clarice might have murdered her husband? I was under the impression he simply skipped town."

"Well, yes, that's the general consensus." Irmajean did like to speculate on the truth and, in her own mind at least, enhance it appropriately. She felt a good story could always be improved upon. In the case of the Carmichael's, there were a lot of gaps to fill.

"What has Priscilla thinking differently?"

"According to stories we've heard, Clarice made a poor choice of husband." Leaning her elbows on the table, Irmajean launched into her favorite subject—Rosewood and its late owners. "She was well into her thirties when she married Bertram Willowby. Brought him home from a world cruise, surprising the whole town because people never thought she'd marry. Apparently things didn't go well right from the start and once Chalmers was born... Anyway, Priscilla has been digging through old boxes and she's run across a lot of stuff belonging to the husband. Boxes and boxes of clothes, books, even a deluxe monogrammed shaving kit. Now what well-groomed man would leave that behind? Especially since we've heard Willowby was something of a dandy."

"Maybe he had more than one shaving kit. One for at home and one for travel."

Irmajean frowned at her husband. "Must you be so reasonable? Doesn't it seem a little unlikely he would leave everything he owned behind?"

"Hon, you don't know that he did. He may have left some things, perhaps with the understanding Clarice would send them on when he got settled."

"Then why didn't she?"

"I can give you several possible reasons…"

Irmajean shook her head. "No, no, I don't want to hear them. Reasonable explanations won't bring in visitors or satisfy them once they get here."

"You're telling me people want scandal."

Irmajean beamed her satisfaction at his understanding. "Exactly."

"Then make something up."

His suggestion shocked her. "People don't want stories, they want the truth."

"Well, since nobody knows the truth..." His tone bordered on exasperation.

"And that's what Priscilla is trying to find out. Honey, even you have to admit it looks a bit strange Willowby was here one day and gone the next."

"When people move on that's usually the case. They don't take themselves off in pieces."

She smiled her satisfaction. "Unless someone else does that for them."

"Irmajean, I've seen pictures of Clarice. She wasn't a beauty by anybody's standards. Not with those thin unsmiling lips, tight knot of hair and ramrod straight back.

But she doesn't look capable of murder. She looks like a woman who would try to do the best with the cards life dealt her. Even if that included a reprobate of a husband."

"Honestly, honey, some days you are absolutely no fun."

"That's not what you occasionally tell me." He waggled his eyebrows.

She gave him a swift kick under the table.

"All kidding aside, you might want to reconsider suggesting to all and sundry that Clarice could have hastened her husband to his grave. Locals still think well of her, particularly the old timers."

Irmajean realized her husband spoke the truth, however much she might not want to hear it. "I won't argue with you, but it would be a real coup if we could discover what did happen to Bertram Willowby. Rosewood is a wonderful old place and it would be a shame to see it close down because of lack of money."

"What happened to the endowment fund Chalmers left?"

Irmajean rested her chin on her hand. "Gone with the wind... Even with a lot of work on the property donated, repairs devoured much of the endowment. A good chunk of money went for the security system Priscilla insisted we needed. She claims the library is really valuable, plus there are many one-of-a-kind antiques. She's applied for numerous grants, but we're still waiting to hear. A nice juicy scandal or even a legitimate mystery would boost visitor appeal. Look at what it's done for the House of Winchester."

"What put Priscilla on the trail of Bertram Willowby anyway? Last I knew, she was looking for a secret entrance into the tower."

"True, but she's rapped and tapped at walls until her knuckles are sore, without a shred of luck. If Clarice sealed off the original staircase as she's rumored to have done, then she did a great job. Common sense suggests there's got to be an entrance other than through the attic, but where it is is the question. Priscilla suggested removing part of the attic wall in search of it, but when she did I thought we'd lose half the board members to apoplexy."

"What about your volunteer secretary, Ted Meyers? Shouldn't he know? Not only has he lived here forever, but he knew Chalmers."

"Actually, they were relatives. His grandfather and Chalmers' grandmother were brother and sister. But Ted pleads ignorance whenever Priscilla questions him. He fidgets so bad, I think he's going to jump out of his skin. Personally, I think he's hiding something."

Glenn looked longingly at his newspaper. "If the subject of Rosewood makes him uncomfortable why do you suppose he volunteers his time there?"

Irmajean picked up her cup and frowned when she saw it was empty. "Good question, one Priscilla and I have pondered over numerous cups of tea. We finally decided it's so he can keep an eye on things." She again propped her chin on her hand. "Rosewood has its secrets we just haven't been able to unlock them. But we will one way or another. You'll see."

"Well," Glenn picked up his paper, "I'm sure you'll find out what you need to. You always do." Then he again lowered his paper. "You know, Irmajean, I think this line of inquiry is—inappropriate. Some questions are better left unanswered."

"*You* tell Priscilla that, because she's not about to let go of this."

"Whatever..." He opened his newspaper and took refuge behind it.

Rosewood being her current favorite topic of conversation, Irmajean was reluctant to end the discussion. But she could tell her husband considered the subject exhausted. "I guess it's time to get going." They'd been away on a three-day weekend and the weeds in Rosewood's garden would have taken advantage of her absence. She pushed herself away from the round oak table situated in a sunny nook of the kitchen. "Are you home today?" Glenn was a real estate appraiser working out of his home office, but he was also on the road a lot.

"I have a house to do in Rockaway, otherwise I am. You want me to start dinner?"

"If you wouldn't mind. Well, then, I guess I'll be off."

Irmajean checked the capacious pockets of her floral garden smock for essentials: gloves, twine, clippers, cat treats, even a pocket flashlight for the deep cabinets in the garden shed. The shed contained everything she might need, but always seemed to be on the opposite side of the garden from where she was. Besides, she reasoned, what else were pockets for if it wasn't for carrying essentials?

Three miles from downtown and a quarter mile off the narrow, twisty Salmonberry Cutoff, Rosewood nestled behind a stand of graceful hemlock trees. The circular drive and covered portico in front were left over from the estate's glory days, when almost every weekend saw the Carmichael's hosting some social event. An era that had ended overnight without explanation. Irmajean burned with curiosity to know the truth of what had happened close to three-quarters of a century ago. She parked her Volvo beside Ted's ancient Plymouth Reliant at the back of the house. Surprisingly, Priscilla's car was nowhere in sight.

She stuck her head into the office located in the basement of the house. Ted hunched over an old Underwood typewriter, hunting and pecking his way through a letter. A state-of-the-art computer system had been donated by a local doctor and Priscilla used it. Ted persisted in banging away on the old relic found stored in Rosewood's carriage house, a repository of odds and ends for over a century.

"Ted, good morning." She forced herself to sound cheerful, determined not to be infected by his habitual sour mood. "Priscilla been in yet?" She asked as she pulled a battered straw hat from its hook by the door.

He glowered at her over his half-glasses. "Not to my knowledge."

"I'm going to get busy in the garden. Pass that on to her when she does come in, will you?" *Did he actually nod in agreement? Honestly*, she thought as she walked from the back of the house toward the three acres of restored garden, *would it kill Ted to at least try and be pleasant?*

A wave of exhilaration always washed over her when she started down Rosewood's garden path. She had her own dear garden at home, complete with comfy garden chairs, tinkling pond, and three snoozing kitties, but Rosewood was so *vast*. It was a horticultural wonder, even with a good two acres of land still overgrown with alder and blackberries. The kind of garden developed when money was no object.

She, along with the rest of the volunteer gardeners, had worked miracles over the last year. When they'd first started reclaiming the property, she'd never have guessed at the plants surviving despite decades of neglect. The only part of the garden Chalmers Carmichael had kept up was the Rose Garden near the house. And that was because it was his mother's favorite. The rest of the property might suffer neglect, but never the roses.

The outdoor property was divided into appropriately named rooms. The Rose Garden led into the Shade Garden, Irmajean's personal favorite. Unfortunately, she knew its shadowy moistness also made it a favorite hang-out for slugs. Nasty, devouring-everything-in-their-path creatures she could annihilate without a twinge of conscience. She'd left off working there last Thursday— had in fact set out some Alchemilla plants and wanted to see how they were doing. They were commonly called Lady's Mantle, but she preferred Alchemilla because it sounded mysterious.

A ring of towering firs and graceful hemlocks presided over this shady corner. Hostas, violets, fuschias and rhododendrons thrived and she loved the moist, woodsy scent hanging in the air. Moss spread like green velvet over smooth stones and crept into the grass walk way. Frederick Blumer, a carpenter and board member, had installed a wooden bench at Irmajean's request. She made for that comfortable spot now.

Irmajean heard a soft meow and glanced down to see Catkin, the eighteen-pound orange tomcat orphaned by the passing of Chalmers Carmichael. Every effort had been made to find him a good home. Efforts he resisted, always eventually finding his way back to Rosewood. Finally Priscilla and the board had decided to let him stay where he was happy, and food and vet bills were figured into the already strained budget. Irmajean had three cats of her own and taking time out for Catkin was no problem. Besides, they both had a mutual antipathy to spending much time in Ted's company.

She felt around in her pockets for a cat treat and held one out for him. He was about to take it when he froze, mesmerized by the top of her head. He'd spotted the stuffed pink bird on her hat. Catkin ignored the proffered treat and so she put it back in her pocket.

"He who hesitates is lost, cat. And no, you can't have my bird."

A slight breeze riffled through the trees and a shower of fir needles drifted into her lap. She sat content a moment, until her wandering gaze came to rest on the Alchemilla bed. She'd set the plants out in a corner that got a certain amount of early morning sun, enough to keep the plants happy. The rest of the day they nestled in shade. Frowning, she rose and walked over to them, dropped to her knees with a slight wince, and tenderly touched bruised, ruffled leaves. Who or what had been digging in the bed? She would have blamed Frederick's ever present canine companion, if the culprit hadn't attempted to replant the plants they'd disturbed. Why would anyone have been digging here? She began clearing the dirt away with her hands, gently lifting aside damaged plants when she heard Ted call her name.

Without even a prick of conscience, she chose to ignore him. Only an extremely pressing complaint would bring him into the garden and she was in no mood to hear what it might be. Ted and whatever drove him into despised territory would keep. She was back in her element and didn't want a dose of him to spoil it.

Not for the first time, she offered up silent thanks to Chalmers Carmichael for dying without heirs and for bequeathing his beautiful estate to the local historical society of which she was an enthusiastic member. And bless his grandmother Rachel for establishing these gardens over a century ago. They'd been sadly neglected, but the restoration process was pure heaven, especially when she discovered some heirloom flower blooming in a patch of weeds. And of course, there were some real treasures among the latter—self heal, plantain, and horsetail, to mention only a few. Rose Campion, one of the other board members, was a trained herbalist who could often be found harvesting plants others might pull up and toss aside.

Once again hearing her name, Irmajean ducked behind an exuberant rhododendron bush. She felt confident Ted would soon abandon his search for her. Watching in fascination, she saw him trip—literally—down the garden path in his haste. Only a good deal of teetering and arm waving kept him from falling face first into a boxwood hedge. "Damn flagstone," he muttered. Then he hesitated, glanced down at his shoes in distaste and repeatedly wiped them on the grass as if he'd stepped in something nasty. Irmajean couldn't help grinning to herself, certain he'd smashed one of the slugs that were the bane of her gardening existence.

Unfortunately, Ted wasn't the only creature prowling the gardens in search of prey. Catkin, having only moments ago disappeared into a patch of ferns, now reappeared on a branch just above Irmajean's head. She caught a glimpse of him out of the corner of her eye, but too late. With ease born from much practice, Catkin sprang through the air and landed squarely atop her head.

The unexpected weight of the cat threw her off balance and she let out a startled yelp while reaching frantically for anything that might keep her from falling. The low hanging branch of a nearby alder barely kept her from toppling over, but not from swaying dangerously to and fro, her balance affected by the cat clinging to her hat. A strap fastened snugly beneath her chin and now it kept the hat and the cat anchored firmly on her head. She'd saved herself from a tumble in the grass, but nothing could save her from Ted. Her cry of surprise had given her away. Catkin, clutching the bedraggled stuffed bird in his mouth, made good his escape, leaving her to watch his flight to freedom with envy.

"There you are," Ted uttered with an ill-disguised note of triumph. "Chief Mallory is at the house and wants to see you."

Her first reaction was one of alarm. Had Glenn met with an accident? "Did he say what he wanted?" Quickly, she attempted to straighten her hat.

"He didn't confide in me. Just sent me to find you. As if I had nothing better to do." Ted emphasized his annoyance with a sniff.

"I'd best see what he wants." Irmajean didn't wait for Ted, quickly losing him as she made use of several shortcuts familiar only to the Friends of Rosewood volunteer gardeners. She found Frank Mallory, Pirate's Cove police chief, pacing the floor of the office, obviously agitated.

"I thought maybe Ted had gotten lost."

"Frank, what brings you out this way?" Irmajean was a trifle breathless from hurrying.

"Is there somewhere we can talk?" The policeman removed his hat and ran a hand through what was left of his hair.

Irmajean could contain her worries no longer. "Has something happened to Glenn?"

"Nothing like that. I didn't mean to give you a scare."

Her relief was obvious. "I could use a cup of tea. Ted isn't apt to follow us to the kitchen. We can talk there." She led the way up a narrow flight of stairs and down a short hallway to a kitchen surprisingly small for a house of Rosewood's size. Without wasting any time, she filled a tarnished copper kettle with water, set it on the stove, then went to a cupboard and took down two heavy mugs and a tin of teabags. "There's not much choice, I'm afraid. Just ordinary black tea. Unless you'd like some instant coffee."

"I'll take the instant."

Irmajean puttered about measuring instant coffee in one cup and dropping a wilted tea bag in another, then pouring water over both once it had boiled. When she placed the mugs on opposite sides of a small pine table with a view of the garden Frank sat down across from her. "I know you're wondering why I'm here."

Irmajean removed her somewhat battered hat and placed it on the table with a pang of regret for her lost bird. "I admit I'm curious."

Frank cleared his throat, while surrounding the thick white mug with his huge hands. "When was the last time you saw Priscilla Norris?"

"Last Thursday. I don't know if your wife mentioned to you that Glenn and I went out of town for a few days. That's why we had to postpone our regular game of bridge with you and Jane. I know Ted saw her on Friday, but she hasn't come in yet today."

"I guess there's no getting around questioning him then." He sighed. "I was hoping to avoid talking to him if I could, but it looks like it's inevitable. He drives me crazy. He's always calling the station and reporting some infraction—his word—of what he considers the law. Complaints that take time away from more important issues. Because, of course, Ted Meyers is Ted Meyers and therefore his complaints take precedence. He never tires of reminding us that his family was among the first in the area. He doesn't seem to get it that nobody cares who his ancestors were."

Irmajean could sympathize with the police chief. Ted, whose feelings were easily hurt, was very high maintenance. But that wasn't the important issue. "Why are you concerned about Priscilla's whereabouts?"

"Her landlady gave us a call this morning. Seems nobody in the apartment complex has seen Ms. Norris in three days. The landlady grew suspicious something might be amiss because she could hear Norris's dog whining. So she used her master key to get into Norris's apartment and discovered the dog was out of food and water and quite obviously hadn't been let outside for sometime. She's pretty upset. Says something has to be wrong because Norris would never neglect her dog."

Irmajean was equally surprised. "Taco was left on his own?"

"Looks that way."

"Priscilla's crazy about that little Chihuahua and brings him to work occasionally. Her landlady was right to be concerned. Priscilla would never go off and leave Taco to fend for himself." She took a long, thoughtful drink of tea and then pushed herself away from the table. "I think we'd better have a chat with Ted. See if he can shed any light on where she might have gone. He should have made his way back to the office by now."

Irmajean snatched up her straw hat before leading the way downstairs. Ted busily ignored them while typing away. Frank cleared his throat twice before Ted, probably peeved over his errand boy status, looked their way. Then the elderly man straightened his wire-rimmed glasses and pursed his lips before saying, "Yes? Is there something *else* I can do for you?"

The corner of Irmajean's mouth twitched and she dared not look at Frank Mallory. Ted would carry the burden of his grudge against the police chief around for days until something else took its place.

Frank ignored the frosty air. "Ted, can you tell me the last time you saw or talked to Priscilla Norris?"

Ted drew himself up huffily. "I haven't seen her since last Friday."

"And you haven't reported it to anyone?"

"Why should I? I'm not her keeper. While her not being here is an inconvenience for me, it's certainly *not* the end of the world. I have my little tasks and they keep me busy. Priscilla is, after all, a grown woman who has never found it necessary to keep me apprised of her comings and goings." Although his tone suggested that in all fairness she should. "Besides, how could I report her missing when I had no idea she was?"

"So you weren't at all worried when she didn't come in today?" Frank prodded.

Ted pursed his lips and attempted to explain. "You must understand that I only work three days a week: Monday, Wednesday and Friday. Priscilla was here on Friday when I left. She said nothing about going anywhere either today or over the weekend. When she didn't come in this morning, I assumed she'd gone somewhere. Usually she leaves me a message of what she wants done. But today there was nothing. Things were much as I'd left them on Friday."

Irmajean knew he spoke the truth. Priscilla was always very exact in her instructions to Ted and the rest of the board members. She had her ideas, and they were very good ones, on how Rosewood should be run. Early on Priscilla had made it clear Ted and the Board of Directors would defer to her, rather than she to them. "After all," she'd said. "You're paying me to direct." She'd always been pleasant to Ted, but her interest and expertise was in the historic preservation of places—not in people. The pioneer status of Ted's family didn't impress her; his crumbling old family house did, but Ted didn't encourage company.

Frank persisted. "But you did see her on Friday?"

Ted nodded. "I left at three p.m. and she was still here."

"And she said nothing about going anywhere?"

"I believe I've already said as much."

Frank folded his beefy arms across his massive chest. "Think, Ted, let me decide whether or not something is important."

Irmajean suspected if Ted knew anything he would now attempt to unearth it. More than anything he longed to be important, he would even interrupt conversations with irrelevant bits of information just so you would notice him. While they waited, she plumbed the depths of her own memory for any seemingly inconsequential snippet of information that might take on new meaning. Priscilla left nothing to chance—certainly not the care of her precious Taco. This circumstance alone made Irmajean twitchy with apprehension and coupled with the fact no one seemed to know where Priscilla was... It suddenly made her extremely aware of anything off-kilter about the day and her thoughts flew to the disturbed state of the Alchemilla plants.

"Would you excuse me for a minute?" She didn't wait for permission but hurried into the garden. Frank didn't need her help to question Ted, and she was sure he'd fill her in on anything of importance the volunteer secretary might have to say.

The Shade Garden was as she'd left it, except the Alchemilla was no longer basking in dappled morning sunlight. She felt a twinge of guilt when she noticed the droopy state of the plants she'd set aside to replant before Ted and Catkin rearranged her morning.

She dropped to her knees and began working the soil with her hands before placing the wilting plants back in the ground. Suddenly their well-being took a back seat when her fingers came into contact with a long, narrow object. Working it free, she sat back on her heels, too puzzled to be apprehensive. Why in the world had someone buried a crowbar in the Alchemilla bed?

Two

Irmajean found herself shaking. It was impossible to dismiss the crowbar as having been there for some time for two reasons. Number one it hadn't rusted, but most important, she'd been digging in this very bed only last week, setting out new plants. The crowbar hadn't been there then. It belonged in the garden shed, not in the Alchemilla bed. Who had buried it there, thinking it safely out of sight? And why? Certainly not a gardener. They would have known another gardener would notice immediately that the plants and soil had been disturbed.

Under ordinary circumstances, she would have been puzzled. But today wasn't ordinary. Priscilla was missing. A spark of intuition warned too late that she probably shouldn't have handled the crowbar, although whoever had buried it would surely have wiped it clean of evidence. You didn't bury a crowbar for any honest reason, did you?

Irmajean struggled to her feet. *Why am I thinking this way,* she wondered? *I don't know that anything bad has happened to Priscilla.* Probably because she read too many mysteries where items and events out of context were catalogued and set aside to be examined as either clues or red herrings. She got to her feet and hastened back to the house, stumbling across the office threshold.

"Come quickly!" she managed between labored breaths. "You need to see what I've found." She noticed Ted's look of relief and assumed Frank's grilling had pushed his comfort zone to its limits.

Frank was at her side. "Show me."

"This way..." She glanced back only once to make certain Frank was keeping up. So much so, he collided with her when she came to an abrupt halt at her destination. "I set some plants out here last Thursday; otherwise I might not have noticed the area had been disturbed. Whoever was responsible tried to put things back as they were, but bruised and wilted plants gave them away."

"Irmajean, I have no idea what you're talking about."

"Never mind, it doesn't matter. I was digging when I found this." She pointed to the crowbar.

"You *just* found this?" With a great deal of effort, Frank knelt down.

Irmajean nodded. "It wasn't there last week. I can swear to that. I thought all things considered you'd want to see it." Then in spite of herself, because she really didn't want to know, she asked, "Do you think it has any connection with Priscilla?"

Knees popping, he stood up and pushed his hat to the back of his head. "Let's hope not. I'll take it into evidence; have the lab check it out. Did you handle it? Of course, you did."

She nodded sheepishly. "Sorry."

"If they find more than one set of fingerprints on it, you'll have to come in. We'll need yours for comparison and elimination."

"I'll be glad to do whatever's necessary." She watched him scan the area.

"What kind of a car did Norris drive?"

The change of subject startled her. "A blue Geo."

"Geez, one of those little cars you could hide in a sock? Are there any buildings on the property where her car could be kept out of sight? It's a stretch I know, but at the moment I don't have anywhere else to go."

Irmajean knew he was considering the worst. The day had started off so beautifully with her joy at being back in Rosewood's garden. How quickly storm clouds of trouble had gathered. She swallowed hard against the lump forming in her throat. "The old carriage house, but it's full to the brim."

"Let's take a look."

"It's kept locked, so we'll have to get the key from the house."

Back at the office, she saw Ted once again hunched over the old Underwood. He ignored her, and she returned the favor while snatching a key from a pegboard holding an abundance of keys.

Frank raised his eyebrows. "They always left out like that?"

Irmajean nodded. "They're pretty accessible, I know. But this seemed easier than issuing every board member and volunteer a key."

"Not exactly tight security. You do lock the outside door when everyone goes home, don't you?" His tone was slightly sarcastic.

"Oh, yes." Ted hastened to reassure him. "It would never do to leave it unlocked all the time. And we turn on the security system Priscilla insisted we have installed. Rosewood is rather isolated..." No sooner were the words out of his mouth than his facial expression gave away the import of what he'd said.

Frank Mallory snorted. "At least we're in agreement there." He shook his head and Irmajean imagined he was cataloguing the flaws in their security, although she didn't know what more they could do.

"Well, let's have a look in that carriage house."

Irmajean led the way through the Rose Garden, bypassing the Spring Garden and vegetable patch where peas and lettuce were already flourishing. Every step of the way she tried to convince herself Frank was only being thorough, that Priscilla had taken a long weekend and Taco had been left in the care of a friend or neighbor who had simply forgotten.

The bushes nearby rustled and Irmajean caught a glimpse of that reprobate, Catkin. Had he eaten her bird? She smiled at the thought, knowing him too smart to be fooled by it for long. She couldn't stay mad at him, even though her head still rang from his assault on her hat. He had too much charm and personality, an opinion shared by visitors to the property. So much so, Priscilla had set out a donation jar for the care and feeding of Rosewood's mascot.

Thoughts of Catkin were banished when they reached the carriage house. The huge padlock hung askew from its latch, eliminating the need for a key.

Ted, apparently more unwilling to be left behind than to entering the garden, had followed them, and now looked dismayed. "*Someone* didn't lock up."

"Priscilla would never have been so careless unless she intended coming right back." Such negligence coupled with Priscilla's absence didn't bode well.

Frank moved forward, pulling the door open. The musty smell of a place long unheated greeted them. "What all's stored in here, anyway?" Hulking shapes loomed, barely illuminated by light filtering through dusty windows.

Ted fluttered his hands. "All sorts of things."

"That doesn't tell me much, Ted."

Irmajean hastened to explain. "After Chalmers died and the historical society was made aware of his legacy, several of us went over the property, including this building. Not box by box mind you, but a general inventory. When Chalmers shut down his newspaper, *The North Coast Explorer*, he moved the entire contents of the office here. I was working for him at the time. He tried donating the old presses and the like to the county museum, but they didn't have room for them. So rather than just junk them he decided to store them here. Plus there are copies of every paper Chalmers, his mother before him and her father before her ever put out. Locals hated to see the paper fold, but Chalmers couldn't find a buyer for it and at sixty-five years old said he'd had it with the newspaper business." Frank had only lived in

Pirate's Cove a couple of years and would have no reason to know much about the late owner of Rosewood. She spread her arms wide. "So here you have stored the entire history of *The North Coast Explorer*."

The interior of the carriage house was like a set for a surrealistic movie. Canvas tarps draped over bulky objects in a vain effort to protect the old newspaper equipment from the insidious inroads of the inevitable rust.

Ted hovered in the entry. Irmajean didn't much like the carriage house either, but followed Frank inside. They peered under every shrouded shape, but discovered nothing that didn't belong. Their search ended at the foot of a flight of stairs.

"What's up there?" Frank asked.

"Boxes of old newspapers and personal items. But look!" And she pointed at the dusty steps.

"I see that. Footprints. Somebody's been up here recently."

"Probably Priscilla. She isn't at all intimidated by dust or dirt, mice or spiders. Which is a good thing since Rosewood has its share of them all."

Frank hesitated at the foot of the wooden stairs. Irmajean hastened to reassure him. "They're sturdier than they look."

"Sure hope so. Are you gonna wait for me down here?"

"Not on your life." She'd rather brave the upstairs with Frank than hover below with Ted. They'd found no sign of Priscilla's car and so far no sign of Priscilla. Irmajean couldn't decide if that was good or bad. The upstairs did show obvious signs someone had been searching through boxes. Papers were strewn everywhere—not at all Priscilla's usual neat style.

"Looks like somebody was in a hurry."

Irmajean walked among the boxes, recognizing labels she'd attached for Chalmers when she was working for him. They conscientiously identified the contents of items from the newspaper. Earlier cartons bore no such identification. These were the ones pulled out from under the eaves and opened; their contents scattered. "Priscilla's constantly looking for more family history. However, it's not like her to leave such a mess, unless something or someone interrupted her. I don't like this at all. Why wouldn't she have tidied this up?"

Frank leaned against a support beam and folded his arms. "You know her far better than I do. So if you say she wouldn't ordinarily have left this mess, I believe you. She might have been called away. We'll know for sure when we find her car. Any other buildings on the property big enough for the Geo?"

"No." Irmajean shook her head. "There are a couple of small sheds where we keep the gardening equipment. But empty they're not big enough for a car, even one as small as Priscilla's."

Frank pushed himself away from the support beam. "We better have a look anyway."

"Frank, you don't really think anything—awful—has happened to Priscilla do you?"

"I'm just making sure she's not anywhere on the property. There's a lot of things that could have happened. She could have fallen and injured herself."

Irmajean knew he spoke the truth, but that kind of accident wouldn't explain the absence of her vehicle.

When they reached the downstairs of the carriage house, it was to find that Ted had abandoned his doorway vigil. "Meyers must have gone back to the house. He's an odd duck if there ever was one."

"He's definitely one of a kind, thank goodness, but I think he feels proprietary toward Rosewood because he and Chalmers Carmichael were friends."

"Is that so? I didn't know that. But then Carmichael was before my time."

"Ted, Chalmers, and Barron Lancaster lunched together every week, regular as clockwork. Three aging bachelors with a passion for Pirate's Cove and its history." She could still see the three of them stationed at *their* table in Dot's Diner.

Irmajean waited while Mallory locked the carriage house.

"I think we should restrict access for now."

Irmajean nodded her agreement. "That seems reasonable." She squinted up at him and he moved to stand between her and the sun. "Are you going to organize a search?"

"Since she hasn't been seen since Friday, you bet. A hungry dog with its legs crossed isn't exactly a missing person report, but given what people have told me about Norris, it's enough for me to take her absence seriously." At that moment his cellphone rang, and he stepped away to answer the call.

Frank's mouth tightened. He obviously didn't like what he was hearing. "Okay, I'll be right there." He snapped his phone shut. "There's a bad accident on 101 just outside of town. I'm needed there. Hang tight and I'll get back to you as soon as I can."

"I'll be here." He didn't exactly tell her *not* to go looking for Priscilla. And since sitting and waiting weren't exactly her strong points, she'd have a look through the house while she killed time.

"You might call the other board members, and see when any of them talked to Norris last. One of them could have the answer we're looking for. Maybe we're worrying about nothing." Then he echoed her thoughts by adding, "Anyway, let's hope so."

"I'll be glad to do that." Irmajean prepared herself to do whatever was necessary in order to settle the mystery of Priscilla's whereabouts. If she could only shake the feeling of dread that had settled over her.

When they reached the house, Irmajean stopped while Frank continued on to his car. "Frank…"

Frank Mallory turned toward her, a questioning expression on his face.

"Frank, do you really think we'll find her?"

"It's not if we'll find her, Irmajean, that's beginning to worry me. But I never give up hope."

Frank's parting words didn't offer her the comfort she craved, and the possibility of misfortune wouldn't let go of her. She'd get busy and go over the house, but first she was going to have a chat with Ted. Maybe she'd be able to get information out of him Frank hadn't.

Ted glowered up at her when she walked into the office. *Oh dear*, she thought. *He's still in a difficult mood. But then, when wasn't he?* She made herself comfortable on the chair beside his desk. "Ted, we need to take Priscilla's absence seriously."

He rested his fingers on the typewriter keys and peered at her over his half glasses. A gesture that always made her feel like she was back in grade school and about to be scolded.

"I thought we were taking it seriously."

She pressed on. "Are you positive you don't know where she might have gone? No one knows more than you about the goings on around here." She wasn't adverse to using a bit of flattery.

Ted preened ever so slightly, but kept silent, which made her want to turn him upside down and shake information out of him. "Are you sure you can't recall Priscilla mentioning an appointment or a trip?"

He responded with a shrug. "How many times do I have to repeat I haven't seen her since last Friday, and she didn't say a word about either an appointment or going away. When I got here this morning, I found the office much as I'd left it. Nothing to suggest anything might be wrong."

Irmajean got to her feet, almost convinced Ted had told all he knew. But she'd known him long enough to be aware he liked to hoard tidbits of information. Could he be doing that now? Since she couldn't immediately prove her suspicions, she supposed there was nothing to do but get on with her search of the house. Then a sudden inspiration seized her. "Perhaps I'll just have a look at her day planner. There might be a clue there." She wondered why she hadn't thought of it sooner.

"Suit yourself." Ted returned to his two fingered assault on the typewriter keys.

Priscilla's desk was neatness itself and her day timer always sat in the center. More than once she'd wondered if Priscilla took a ruler and measured its exact location from each end of the desk. Irmajean felt it was a metaphor for the precise way Priscilla conducted her life. A preciseness that made her absence so unsettling.

She picked up the leather-covered volume and opened it to a place marked by one of Priscilla's business cards. "The space for last Friday is blank. So is the weekend. There's a notation jotted down for today however." She spoke aloud, suspecting Ted was interested even if he pretended otherwise.

There was no mistaking Priscilla's boldly neat handwriting or what she'd written—however puzzling. *IJ back—tell her about the maze.*

Irmajean turned to Ted with excitement. She and Priscilla had run across a book in Rosewood's extensive library chronicling the history of mazes and labyrinths. In the chapter covering the Hampton Court garden maze in England, someone had written in the margins suggesting a similar maze might have been planned at Rosewood. They'd come across no further evidence of one, but it had been fun to speculate. Had Priscilla found proof? Two acres of the estate were still so overrun by blackberries you couldn't tell what had once been there. Excitement over the possibility almost nudged aside the fear she had for Priscilla's safety—almost, but not quite. "Ted, can you shed any light on what she might have meant?" She really wanted to say, *Come on, Ted, Loosen up*, but refrained.

Ted removed his glasses and began polishing them. A gesture he often made when a situation or comment made him uncomfortable. "A maze? I have no idea."

Irmajean prodded. "Are you sure? You've lived here forever, you must know if there was a garden maze and where it was located."

"You'll have to ask Priscilla when she returns, what she meant." He continued polishing his glasses.

Honestly, he couldn't be more exasperating if he tried. Didn't he realize what a roadblock his obstinacy was?

"Ted, why do you refuse to share your knowledge of the past? I don't buy the excuse you don't know or you don't remember." She fixed him with what she hoped was an intimidating glare.

Ted's watery eyes widened and his mouth tightened, but he said nothing, simply continued cleaning his glasses until one of the lenses popped out.

Irmajean couldn't help smirking. She felt she'd hit a nerve of truth with her accusation as Ted stood there eyeing his broken glasses. Confident she'd get no help from him, she set off to search the house, tramping with determination up the back stairs to the kitchen. It was a small room with no wasted space. Definitely a one-person kitchen. She opened the door to the dumbwaiter, stuck her head inside, but other than an old house smell, she noticed nothing out of the ordinary.

The rest of the main floor contained a living room, formal dining room, large entry, library and a bathroom. Antiques gleaned from the upstairs now furnished the downstairs. Irmajean recalled the threadbare furniture in place when the historical society took possession.

Chalmers had replaced nothing, and if faded squares on the carpet were any indication, he probably hadn't ever rearranged a stick of furniture. She'd liked Chalmers, found him a considerate employer, but he'd been as fussy in many ways as Ted.

The best cared for room in the house had been the library. Books crammed floor to ceiling shelves, many of them out-of-print volumes on local history. In contrast to the rest of the house, Chalmers must have dusted this room and its contents regularly. Its spotless condition suggested he had been a devoted book collector.

There was nothing out of place as far as she could tell about the main floor, other than an unwashed teacup in the kitchen sink. And that was evidence of nothing more than an individual too lazy to tidy up after themselves.

What had she expected, she wondered, as she climbed the elaborate oak staircase to the second floor, passing beautiful beveled and stained glass windows. The windows themselves had been a bit of a puzzle until a recent visitor pointed out many of the cryptic designs were Masonic symbols. Now she wished someone could explain the strange engravings on all the door hinges.

She carefully inventoried the three large bedrooms, bath, and two smaller rooms on the second floor. The latter were barely big enough for a single bed each and so plainly decorated, that Priscilla speculated they might once have been occupied by servants. Irmajean thought they looked like a converted closet tucked away as they were in a corner. Perhaps that's what they'd been originally.

A huge cupboard against the wall narrowed the hallway, and she pulled in a deep breath to ease her passage. She was after all, a trifle well padded in places. It remained a mystery how the heavy, freestanding cabinet had been moved upstairs in the first place. Could it have been constructed where it sat? It weighed so much they couldn't even scoot it away from the wall to see behind it. At the end of the hall and running in back of the cupboard wall, was a steep, enclosed staircase to the attic. Irmajean loved Rosewood, but she did not like the attic or the claustrophobic stairway leading up to it. She hesitated, as she always did, at the foot of these stairs, peering up into the drafty darkness of the unfinished attic. It was one of Priscilla's favorite places and she claimed it contained the answers to the questions concerning Rosewood's secrets. As far as Irmajean was concerned, it only contained mice, spiders and once to her chagrin, a swooping bat that chased her down the stairs.

Gathering her courage, Irmajean climbed the narrow treads, stopping at the top to catch her breath and let her eyes adjust to the lack of light. Sniffing, she thought the attic smelled worse than usual. A naked light bulb dangled from the raftered ceiling and she inched toward it, careful not to step off the boards laid from beam to beam. She didn't want to go crashing through the ceiling. She pulled the string and then waited while the bulb flickered on, then off, then on again. The attic became only a little less sinister as the corners remained shadowed. Mice rustled in newspapers stored in a far corner, and a draft from a hole under the eaves brushed the back of her neck, making her shiver. This part of the house gave her the creeps, and she had to force herself not to run for the stairs. Pulling out her pocket flashlight, she shone its narrow beam into the darkened corners. A pair of tiny eyes reflected back at her. She wrinkled her nose and supposed the unpleasant odor could be blamed on mice. Sniffing again, she ventured it would be more accurate to say dead mice. Maybe Frederick Blumer could be persuaded to clean out the nests. Like Priscilla, he didn't seem to be daunted by anything.

She crept across the wobbly plank flooring, until she stood outside the entrance to the tower sunroom. The location of this room was one of Rosewood's anomalies. It contained vintage wicker furniture, now gnawed by rodents, long dead plants, and the corpses of hundreds of flies and bees. Obviously, this sunny room had been a favorite spot, but now the only access was through the dark, unfinished attic. An unlikely situation. Priscilla surmised at one time another entrance—logically a staircase from the ground floor—had existed. Finding it proved to be another matter. At a recent board meeting, Priscilla had suggested they open up the only finished wall outside of the sunroom itself and see if it hid a staircase. After all, she'd argued, there had to be some reason why only the one wall had been finished. The board of directors, with the exception of Irmajean, had responded with horror at even the thought of such vandalism.

The sunroom and this short wall were finished in bead board with a skinny passage barely wide enough for Irmajean to turn around; even then, she brushed the walls separating the two. Here a permanent section of flooring had been nailed down. Priscilla had taken one look at this protruding wall and proclaimed it the logical site for a staircase.

Taking a couple of steps while shinning her light into the narrow passage, she noticed boards cluttering the floor. They were obviously part of the bead board wall. Puzzled, Irmajean moved her light upward and gasped. Where there'd been solid paneling, there was now a gaping hole. *Oh, my,* she thought. *This was not good. The board members would have a fit.* Then she caught her breath and grimaced. The peculiar, unpleasant smell was stronger here. Was there a worse problem than mice? Perhaps rampant dry rot? No, Glenn said it smelled like cat urine.

Curiosity drew her closer, even though the odor nauseated. She hesitated to stick her head through the hole. Except how else would she know what was in there? Extending the beam of her light into the opening, she saw a spiraling flight of stairs. Oh, my God, Priscilla was right. Bracing herself with one hand against the wall, Irmajean leaned into the break. Within seconds, she recoiled backward, hitting her head on the jagged top of the hole and probably drawing blood, although she hardly noticed or cared. A twisted, bloated shape lay on the stairs, caught in an unnatural position. She'd glimpsed reddish gold; the exact shade of Priscilla's fly away hair.

Her heart pounded, but she had to look again, to make certain of what she saw. Even though she wanted nothing more in the world than to be wrong. Gathering up what little courage remained, Irmajean forced herself to peer once again into the opening. She'd made no mistake. It *was* Priscilla. And now, Irmajean saw the wide open staring eyes, the dried blood marring one side of her face, the early signs of putrefaction. It was all too horrible. It was all too real.

"Oh no," she kept repeating. "Oh, no, oh, no, oh, no." And she burst into tears. Priscilla was vindicated in her belief there was a staircase. Unfortunately, the lovely, quirky, energetic young woman had paid for the discovery with her life.

Three

Irmajean had stopped crying, but she couldn't stop shaking and stumbled several times on the stairs—all three flights of them. Ted looked up from typing, started to speak and then stopped mid-word.

"Call—" her voice was a hoarse croak. "Call 911! Hurry!"

Ted sat there looking at her, his mouth hanging open.

Irmajean made her way over to the chair by his desk and collapsed. "Stop gaping at me and call 911! Now!" Her voice was shaking as badly as her legs, and Ted sat there with his mouth hanging open and his eyes wide with alarm. At the end of her patience, she reached across him, fumbled with the phone and finally managed to get hold of it and place the call herself.

Things happened quickly then, and she supposed Frank had been on his way back to Rosewood when her call came through. He'd be angry with her, annoyed at the very least, that she'd ignored his request to call the board members and instead had gone over the house. She was more than a little annoyed with herself. She would have given almost anything not to have been the one to find

Priscilla. To have her final lasting memory of her young friend be what she'd just seen—was unthinkable. And yet there was no going back.

"Irmajean. Irmajean."

She blinked and turned to find Frank Mallory kneeling beside her. She hadn't even heard him come in.

"You want to tell me what's going on?"

"I found her…"

Frank got to his feet, and bless him, didn't ask who. "Where is she?"

"Upstairs—in the attic. She's—she's had a terrible accident."

He turned to Ted. "Care to show me the attic?"

Ted's eyes widened in alarm. "Oh, I couldn't. No—I couldn't!"

Irmajean squeezed her eyes shut tight. Could she face the attic, knowing what was up there? She couldn't expect Frank to wander around looking for the three flights of stairs. Did she have a choice? She struggled to her feet even though the lead surrounding her heart weighed her down. "I'll show you."

"No," and Frank's large hand pushed her back into her chair. "Ted can show me."

Irmajean glanced at Ted and saw he was trembling. She couldn't subject him to the nightmare in the attic. Despite the pressure of Frank's hand on her shoulder, she managed to stand. "It's better if I show you."

"Sure you're up to it?"

No, she thought, but said nothing, merely nodded. She didn't glance at Ted or at Frank, trusting he needed no encouragement to follow her. The steps up from the basement to the kitchen seemed steeper than usual.

"Irmajean, are you sure you're up to this?"

"I know for sure Ted isn't."

"You could have given me directions." He huffed and puffed behind her.

"No, this attic is a dangerous place." The appropriateness of her words hit home only after the fact, and she hastened to explain. "For some reason we've yet to figure out, an actual floor was never laid down in the attic except in a small area."

"You mean we're gonna have to crawl across beams?"

"Not quite that bad. There are boards laid beam to beam, but they're not nailed down. Priscilla wanted Frederick Blumer, the board member who's also a carpenter, to put down a floor, but he argued against it. Claimed it would spoil the original integrity of the house." She paused at the foot of the attic stairs. "I smelled something—off. Thought it was probably mice. I can't believe I was so stupid, but then I had no idea..."

"And why should you?"

"I just hope she didn't suffer—lying twisted and injured—hoping someone would come along—and then when they didn't..." She was not ashamed of the tears blurring her words.

Frank touched her arm. "Look, I can take it from here. Why don't you wait in one of those rooms? I won't be long, then I'll call in the paramedics. I just want to make sure it was an accident."

Irmajean, glanced at the rooms he indicated. Of course, he couldn't know how small they were, only big enough for a narrow bed and bureau. With the door shut, it would feel like a box—or some other confining place. She thought of the twisted shape trapped in the old staircase.

"No, I can't wait down here."

Frank shook his head, "Okay, whatever you want." He followed her up the steep staircase and cautiously across the wobbly boards. Once they reached the desecrated wall, he took command. "That bare bulb the only light?"

"'Fraid so." She watched as he pulled his flashlight from his belt. Then he squeezed past her and she waited for his verdict. It seemed to take him forever, and she was surprised when he eased his large frame through the opening and on to the stairs. When he emerged, she could tell little from his expression, but then the lighting was poor. He said nothing, just looked down at his feet and then at her.

"I'm gonna have to ask you to leave the attic and keep anyone other than my team away."

"Okay…"

"I mean it. I don't want anyone who doesn't belong up here."

"What's going on, Frank? Did I miss something?"

He gave a hitch to his gun belt. "This was no accident, and this is now officially a crime scene."

Irmajean felt exactly as she had the one time someone persuaded her to ride a roller coaster. As if everything inside had dropped to her feet. She was momentarily speechless, horrified at what he'd said. "You can't be serious."

"Believe me, I am."

"But who would want to hurt Priscilla?"

"That's what we're gonna have to find out."

Irmajean grabbed hold of the word *we*, even though she knew Frank didn't intend including her. She was not about to be shut out, intended instead doing everything she could to see Priscilla's killer brought to justice.

"Let's get downstairs. I've got to call for back up, and you and Ted need to close the house. I don't want anybody in here except my crime team. Understand?"

"Do you still want me to call the other board members?"

"I do, but I don't want you to say anything about what's happened to Priscilla. Tell them there's a meeting at nine tomorrow morning and they're all to be here. I'm hoping I can keep the news from leaking out until then. I'd like to see their various reactions when they hear Norris was murdered."

"Do you really think you can keep it quiet until then?"

"I'm sure as hell gonna try."

When they reached the office, Ted was sitting at his typewriter, his fingers resting on the keys, his eyes watching the stairs.

"Ted, Frank wants everyone here for a nine a.m. board meeting tomorrow."

Frank pointed his finger at Ted. "And I don't want a single word of what went on here today leaked to anyone. Hear me?"

Ted, his faded blue eyes widening, nodded. Irmajean noticed he was still trembling and almost felt sorry for him, but she couldn't stop her own inner trembling.

She was able to talk to three of the board members, but had to leave messages for the rest. The task finished, she looked over to find Ted watching her. He shook like a man terrified, but his expression was one of bewilderment. Then she realized no one had actually told him what was going on. "Ted, Priscilla is dead. And Frank thinks she was murdered."

A kaleidoscope of expressions moved across Ted's face, and she could understand his confusion, but not his ultimate reaction.

"What will happen to Rosewood now?"

Irmajean was momentarily speechless. Murder! A word that sounded as violent as its meaning and yet, Ted's first response was to ask about the future of the house. Was that because he was concerned about his own future? His volunteer work at Rosewood seemed the focal point of Ted's life. How sad to have crept into old age with no other attachments, and she thought fondly of her husband, their three cats and their thirty-two year old twin daughters, Gemma and Chloe. The abruptly ended life in the attic made her more aware than ever of her own good fortune. She thought how a shared tragedy brings people closer and she sought to reassure Ted. "I imagine the board will hire a new director. But whatever Ted, you'll be needed. Rosewood can't run without its volunteers." Which was certainly true enough. "I think there are enough of us who care about the property to keep it going in a way to satisfy the terms of Chalmers' will." She knew as well as Ted that the property was to be sold if the historical society no longer felt up to managing it.

Her answer seemed to appease Ted, and he went away as close to happy as he ever managed. She'd always thought Ted a man born in the wrong time, someone who didn't quite fit. Volunteering at Rosewood gave him a place where the past reigned. Where his dusty clothes, wire rimmed glasses and stooped shoulders seemed right at home. She shook her head while watching Ted shamble to his car. Was he an anachronism by accident or design?

The rest of the local police force arrived on the heels of Ted's departure. Irmajean didn't ask for permission to remain on the property. Even though Priscilla had been a contemporary of her daughters, she and the much younger woman had been friends. Sharing a passion to see Rosewood returned to the splendor of its glory days. There would be no replacing her even if they found someone else as committed to preserving the property. But would they? Despite her reassurances to Ted, Irmajean had her doubts. Priscilla kept enthusiasm for the property alive. In the wake of her death, the less enthusiastic members of the historical society might move to shut Rosewood down and put the property on the market. After all, the legacy was a huge responsibility and it took a lot of money and a host of volunteers to keep it going.

Fifteen minutes hadn't passed when Irmajean glanced up from her musings to see Ted standing pale and shaken in the doorway. She jumped up, knocking the chair over in the process and startling the cat she didn't realize was curled up on the filing cabinet behind her.

"Ted, what's happened?" His ghastly expression left her in no doubt that something horrific had taken place.

Ted swallowed in an effort to loosen the tightness in his throat. "Her car." His voice was an appalling croak.

"Priscilla's car... I found it. I mean I didn't go looking for it, but I found it."

"Ted, take a deep breath. Then tell me where."

He clutched at his chest; unaware beads of perspiration dotted his forehead.

"Ted, are you going to be all right?"

"I was headed home and I don't drive very fast."

"Yes, I know." Neither did Irmajean, but she'd gotten behind Ted once too often when she couldn't pass and always wondered if either of them would live long enough to reach their destination. Ted lived five miles beyond Rosewood. "What did you see?"

"Priscilla's car... Backed off the road... Nothing visible except its two little headlights like eyes peering up from over the bank—shattered just like the windows were shattered. I came back here to tell you. So you could tell Chief Mallory." His frequent pauses and the way he clutched his chest alarmed her. As long as she'd known Ted, he'd never seemed the picture of health and right now, he was as gray as his remaining wisps of hair.

"Ted, sit down!" She all but pushed him into a chair. "Take a deep breath and try to relax. I'm going to go up to the kitchen and make you a cup of tea. The police don't want to be interrupted right now."

He gave her a panicked look as if he might fly apart if she left him alone.

"I'll be back within minutes. I'm just going up to the kitchen and I'll be able to hear you if you need me."

Ted stumbled to his feet. "I'll come with you." He followed her so closely that he stepped on her heels—twice.

After putting water on to boil and dropping a tea bag in a cup, she turned her full attention to Ted. "Are you going to be okay?"

"It was vicious. Just vicious."

She sat the tea in front of him and he gulped down a drink, only to have it dribble onto his tightly buttoned sweater when he realized it was too hot.

Irmajean grabbed a tea towel and mopped at his sweater. "What was vicious, Ted?"

The little man raised watery eyes to stare at her. "That anyone would smash the windows and the lights the way they did. Wasn't it enough to run the car off the road? Wasn't it enough they'd already destroyed Priscilla? Did they have to destroy her car too?" He held his cup in both hands and took a tentative sip. "Someone must have hated Priscilla a great deal."

Irmajean thought of the twisted, battered body in the attic wall and nodded. "Yes, yes, I would have to say you're right." *But who? Was it some stranger?* No, she was very afraid it was someone they knew. The far corners of the attic was not a likely place to rendezvous with a stranger. She was not inclined to suspect Ted. He was never good at hiding his feelings, and he was obviously devastated by his discovery. Whoever had maimed Priscilla's car, it wasn't Ted.

Ted drained his cup and set it clattering in the saucer. "Priscilla was so fond of that little car."

"You're positive it was hers?"

"I knew it was her car because of the crystal dangling from the mirror. I was driving behind her once and the sunlight glinting off it was quite blinding. I said as much to her, but she informed me it kept the flow of energy moving in a positive fashion, and she wasn't about to remove it. Have you ever heard of such a thing?"

Irmajean nodded, but said nothing. She doubted Ted would understand her explanation any more than he had Priscilla's.

Ted glanced at her pleadingly. "Do you think it will be long before the Chief comes downstairs? I'm really not feeling too well."

"I have no idea." She told him then inspiration seized her. "Why don't you show me where you found the car? Then you can get on home and I can relay the information to Frank."

Several years seemed to slip from Ted's countenance as he nodded in agreement. "Will you drive?"

She was about to suggest following him, but saw he was still too upset to drive. *And I'm not?* Surprisingly, calm settled over her and distress was replaced by a quiet determination to do what had to be done.

Ted clutched the car seat with one hand and the door with the other. He shook as if from cold and yet perspiration beaded his brow.

"How come didn't you notice the car when you came to work this morning or on another trip to town?" For that matter, she wondered why somebody else hadn't reported the car. The Salmonberry Cutoff road wasn't a thoroughfare, but it got its share of traffic.

Ted cleared his throat, but his voice still came out as a hoarse squeak. "I went home right after leaving Rosewood on Friday, and I haven't left my house until I came to work this morning. I remember distinctly meeting a log truck coming around that corner. They really take their share of the road and more and the Salmonberry Cutoff isn't designed for that. Besides, it's a mass of blackberry bushes and I think they must have kept Priscilla's car from rolling into the river."

Would Ted have any reason not to tell her the truth? Irmajean knew the people who lived along the Salmonberry were always complaining about the log trucks, and so Ted's explanation seemed legitimate enough. He was a prig, but he was also conscientious.

"There! Right there!" He waggled his fingers in the direction of a tight curve. The curve was sharp and any cautious driver would be concentrating on their driving. She saw how he could have missed the car on his way to work, especially if meeting a log truck.

"Ted, I want you to stay put." There wasn't much room to pull off, so Irmajean turned on her flashers before climbing out of the car. She knew Priscilla wasn't in her vehicle, but nevertheless she skidded down the bank to examine the Geo.

Ted was right. Somebody had put the car in neutral, pushed it down the bank—probably hoping it would roll into the river, only to have the wattled blackberry vines stop it. Prior to that, they'd smashed everything they could smash and carved the cushions to pieces. It was a nasty job that must have been done at night when there was little traffic on the road; otherwise, someone would surely have witnessed the crime in progress. It looked as if the anger and hate that snuffed out Priscilla's life had lasted long enough to vandalize her small car. Whatever had Priscilla done to provoke such violence?

Hearing a vehicle approach, then slow down, Irmajean glanced up toward the highway. A rattletrap of a pickup, with rust spots the size of dinner plates and the bumper hanging askew, pulled up behind her Volvo. A man, probably in his mid to late thirties, with bright orange dreadlocks and a matted beard got out and walked over to the edge of the road.

"Hey, Dude! Whatcha' doin'?"

She'd been called a good many things, but never dude. "Checking this car out." Irmajean started to work her way back up to the road, being careful not to grab any blackberry vines or devil's club on the way. "Have you by any chance noticed it before?"

The stranger extended a calloused hand and pulled her the last few feet to level ground. "Can't say I have. Not here anyway, but it looks like the car the chick who works at Rosewood drives. I've seen it parked there often enough. Or one just like it. Hey, you might want to check with her." Then the condition of the car seemed to dawn on him. "She isn't in there, is she?"

"No, no she isn't." She peered at him closely. He was not someone you'd ever overlook. Did that mean he was new in town? "Do you live up this road? Or are you just passing by?"

"Yeah, I live in a trailer a coupla miles off the highway. I'm a roofer. Lots a buildin' goin' on around here. Keeps me busy. Keeps a roof over my head." And he laughed heartily at his own joke.

Irmajean couldn't help grinning. Like a lot of real characters, this guy was likable. No doubt he thought her the odd one. She extended her hand. "We've never met. I'm Irmajean Lloyd. I volunteer at Rosewood."

"Name's Karl Webster and I live a couple of miles up Salal Road. I've heard all about you from Teddy."

Irmajean raised an eyebrow. "Teddy?"

"Yeah, Ted Meyers and I are neighbors. I grow me a big garden and share it with him. Ole Teddy likes his veggies." Karl ducked down and looked in Irmajean's vehicle. "Hey, that's Teddy you've got in there." Karl rapped on the window and waved at Ted Meyers who barely lifted his hand in chagrined acknowledgement.

Irmajean didn't know when she'd seen a less likely pair of buddies. But for some odd unexplainable reason, she was glad Ted had such a friend.

"Nice to meet ya." He scratched, spit, and headed back to his truck. Leaving Irmajean to wonder what momentary aberration had driven reclusive Ted Meyers to rent trailer space to the likes of Karl Webster. He seemed likable enough, but maybe that was only his public persona. She'd seen Ted cringe when Karl tapped on the car window and she tried to recall if there'd been something more than a touch of embarrassment on Ted's face— perhaps fear.

Four

Ted Meyers wasn't quite sure how he got himself home. He couldn't remember when he'd been so relieved to see his own front door. Even if Karl Webster was sitting on the steps, his almost fluorescent orange dreadlocks visible even in the settling twilight. Ted wondered with an inward groan what the young man could possibly want and regretted the impulse that had prompted him to let Karl move onto his property. Ted had discovered the hard way that inviting someone in was a good deal easier than dislodging them.

Karl's camp was a quarter of a mile from the house, and they didn't see that much of one another, but it was the idea his home was no longer entirely his own. In all fairness, Karl seldom took advantage of the situation. He'd wanted a place to live rent-free and Ted had been willing and able to provide that. Had even felt he owed Karl that much. But tonight he was in no mood for any company beyond that of a good stiff drink.

Karl got to his feet with an agility Ted had often envied. "Teddy, you okay? You didn't look so good when I saw you earlier."

Ted winced, knowing an explanation was in order. "No, no I'm fine." He pulled a handkerchief from his pocket and mopped his brow. "There's been some trouble up at Rosewood." He felt safe admitting that much since Karl knew the condition of Priscilla's car.

"Trouble beyond that vehicle pushed off the road?"

Ted nodded.

"You gonna tell me or are we gonna play twenty questions?"

"Do I have a choice?"

Karl patted him on the back. "Of course you do, Teddy. Of course you do. Life is one big choice."

Contrary to his first reaction, Ted realized that he did want to talk with someone. He pushed open the door and said, "Let's go inside, I could use a drink." Ted allowed himself a sherry every evening after dinner. But this evening he felt he couldn't wait. The pounding in his chest had subsided and the feeling of dizziness, but he still needed a shot of courage.

Karl trailed along behind him, feeling as he always did when he entered Teddy's house that he was stepping back in time. Everything about the interior was dark. Dark lighting, dark wallpaper, dark wainscoting, heavy dark mahogany furnishings. Karl doubted Teddy had ever changed a thing, leaving it just as his mother had designed it. No wonder Teddy was such a fussy old maid. Karl knew he'd lose his mind in a week if he had to live with that maroon wallpaper. And the draperies, they were never opened. Hard to tell what was probably living in them by now. He'd often wondered what Ted was so afraid of?

Karl detoured in the direction of the kitchen, going to the refrigerator and helping himself to a beer. He didn't have any refrigeration at his place, and Teddy didn't seem to mind that he kept a few brews chilled. He watched in surprise as the old guy poured and then downed in one gulp his daily allotment of alcohol. Teddy's hands were shaking like he had palsy and his color, never very good, was non-existent. "Hey, Teddy, why don't you go sit down, and I'll rustle us up some cheese and crackers. You shouldn't be drinkin' on an empty stomach."

"Another sherry. I'll have another sherry." And Ted licked his lips.

"Whatever you say. Just go sit down and I'll take care of everything." Something pretty awful must have happened to put the old boy in such a flap. Karl washed his hands and then set about slicing some cheese, an apple, and opening a packet of crackers. He arranged these along with another glass of sherry on a tray. Teddy liked things done with a certain amount of style.

Karl set the tray down on a side table and then parked himself on a tufted ottoman. "Okay, Teddy, what happened today? And don't tell me nothin' because one look at you dispels that notion."

Ted nibbled at a piece of cheese like a cautious mouse. "If I tell you, you must promise me you won't say anything to anybody. The police want things kept quiet as long as possible."

"Mum's the word, ole buddy. You know darn well I can keep a secret." His gaze met Ted's, and they locked in understanding.

"Priscilla, Miss Norris... Oh, God!" And he buried his head in his hands. It was only seconds before he felt Karl's hand on his shoulder.

"Easy there. It can't be that bad."

"It's the worst..." Then he remembered another time, another incident and knew that while Priscilla's death was terrible, it wasn't the worst thing he'd ever experienced. His shoulders slumped. "She's dead. *Murdered!*"

Karl felt a sharp twist in his gut. He'd never seen Teddy so upset, and he knew it wasn't because the old guy was particularly fond of Priscilla Norris. He knew a lot of Teddy's secrets, but he sure as heck didn't know them all. To be this upset almost suggested a certain involvement, but he didn't think Teddy had the gumption to kill somebody. "You sure about that?"

Ted nodded and took another gulp of sherry. "I'm sure. The police have been there all afternoon." Ted poured himself another drink.

"Better go a little easy there, Teddy."

Ted ignored the advice. "I can't believe this is happening. Something like this happens once, and you think it can never happen again. Then it does."

"What are you gettin' at?" Suspicion underlined Karl's question.

Ted glanced up, surprise in his expression as if he'd forgotten who he was with. "Something—happened a long time ago. Too long ago to matter now."

"That's a pretty lame explanation from a guy who's guzzled a week's ration of booze in less than fifteen minutes." And he chugged a good half of his bottle of beer while never taking his eyes off Ted. "Any idea who might have had it in for her?"

Ted shook his head. "None. She liked to keep us all on our toes—show us she was boss." He took another swig of sherry then added grudgingly, "But she was good at her job."

"Somebody obviously didn't like her."

Ted spoke to himself more than to Karl. "Irmajean said Priscilla had been going through boxes in the carriage house. Maybe she found something she shouldn't have." He knew darn well that was the truth. She'd found the old staircase, hadn't she? Walled up for over sixty years, and now it was the death of her. Sometimes he thought a curse hung over Rosewood. Sometimes he thought a curse hung over him.

"Where'd they find her body?"

"In the attic. Shoved inside an old staircase that was walled up."

"Then how'd she get inside?" Karl scratched his mangy looking beard.

"Someone—maybe Priscilla herself—had torn the boards from the wall."

"Jeez, sounds like something out of Nancy Drew."

Ted didn't have a chance to answer when someone knocked at the front door. "Oh, my God. This is Monday evening."

Karl knew without asking what that meant. Monday nights Teddy, Barron Lancaster and Chalmers Carmichael when he was alive, met for dinner and conversation. Karl got to his feet. "I'll let him in on my way out. This living room isn't big enough for both of us. Can't see why you put up with him. He treats you like..." Karl shook his unkempt dreadlocks.

He opened the door to Barron Lancaster then pushed past him. "Teddy's in the living room." With that parting remark, he was down the stairs and headed for his truck when he spotted another car coming up the drive. He thought he recognized the Volvo he'd seen earlier. When Irmajean Lloyd eased out of the car, he walked toward her.

"Lookin' for Teddy?"

"I was worried about him. Wanted to make certain he got home all right. But I can see everything is well in hand because you're here, and no one else in town drives a Mercedes except Barron Lancaster."

"Oh, yeah. He shows up regular as clockwork every Monday night."

"Well, I suppose I'll head on home." Then she hesitated. "I do need to talk to Barron. Do you suppose they'd mind?" She hadn't been able to reach him earlier, and she wanted to make certain he understood the importance of tomorrow's board meeting.

"Hey! The door's open. You won't be interrupting anything. They might even offer you a glass of sherry if Teddy hasn't emptied the bottle."

Irmajean grimaced.

"Yeah, my thoughts exactly. Feel free to help yourself to one of my beers in the fridge." With a wave of his hand, he was off.

Irmajean hesitated. She hated to interrupt, but curiosity did get the better of her. She'd never been inside Ted's home, and she did want to speak to Barron. Throwing caution to the wind, she marched up the stairs, rapped on the door and when it swung open, stepped cautiously inside. She could hear voices coming from what she supposed was the living room and moved in that direction.

Ted, Chalmers and Barron had seemed an unlikely trio. But they were not only from pioneer families, but pioneer families with ties of friendship and blood. Chalmers' grandfather, Barron's grandmother and Ted's grandmother had been brother and sisters. She was about to call out when she heard Barron's voice.

"Don't bother to get up, Ted. I can help myself to a whiskey just as I've done for more years that I can count. What did young Webster want?"

"He was just checking on me."

Lancaster raised a questioning eyebrow. "Such solicitous behavior. You're quite lucky to have such a— neighbor."

Ted drained his glass of sherry. "Yes, I suppose I am." Although he knew Barron had meant his comment facetiously, he would take it at face value. He never had been, never would be, a verbal match for Barron Lancaster. When Barron had chosen the law for a profession, he had chosen well. Where Ted had relied on the careful management of inherited money for his livelihood. The few people who had ever come to the house thought he kept it as a shrine to his mother's memory. The truth was he couldn't afford the extravagance of redecorating. He had tried various jobs over the years, but none of them had been very successful. And so, he carefully stretched the money that had been left him, hoping against hope that he wouldn't outlive it.

Barron sat across from him in the chair Ted had come to think of as Barron's chair. The lawyer's long legs stretched toward the fireplace, although tonight the hearth was cold. A fire would have been nice and even though it was May, not unwelcome. Spring so far had been wet and colder than usual. He should have asked Karl to build one. Perhaps he would have if Barron hadn't arrived when he did. Ted was very much aware that neither Webster nor the aging attorney cared for one another. He knew why Barron didn't like Karl, but he'd never been able to get the younger man to admit what he didn't like about Lancaster. Oh, well, it probably didn't matter. Karl's presence on his property was proving to be a mixed blessing. He hadn't known quite what to expect when the young man moved in with his camp trailer. As he considered the unlit fire, he realized just how much Karl did for him and how he was coming to depend on him. He knew Barron would advise against it, but Ted was finding a certain pleasure in no longer being alone. It was at times like these that he missed Chalmers the most. He was far more approachable than Barron. What would his late friend have had to say about Karl Webster?

Lancaster turned his glass of whiskey slowly in his slender, well-manicured hands. Even at seventy-eight he still cut an impressive figure and knew it. "Did you work at Rosewood today?"

"Yes." Careful, he thought, remembering Frank Mallory's edict of silence.

Barron held his glass to his cheek. "Then you must know why all the police cars are there."

"I really can't say."

Barron frowned. "Can't or won't?"

"You'll know soon enough." Then he tensed, wondering how Barron would react to this show of backbone. Barron had always made him feel as if everything he said and did was up for question. As if his shoes were on the wrong feet or his pants unzipped.

"Am I to understand you're refusing to tell me?"

"I can't tell you. There's a difference." The narrow-eyed glare his old friend shot him, almost made him cave in. But much as he respected Barron, he respected the authority of the chief of police more. And Frank Mallory had told him to say nothing. Barron took another sip of his whiskey. "There was a message on my answering machine from Irmajean about a board meeting tomorrow. Can I trust I'll discover this big secret then?"

Ted nodded miserably, then threw Barron a crumb of information he didn't think fell under the edict of silence. "Priscilla had been rummaging through some old boxes stored in the carriage house and was excited about what she'd found." Here Ted shivered. "She found something I'd actually succeeded in forgetting."

"What was that?" There was a sharp edge to Barron's question suggesting he wasn't as immune to the things bothering Ted as he wanted Ted to think.

Ted removed his glasses and rubbed his eyes. He recalled the yellowed, musty smelling roll of papers Priscilla had triumphantly brandished in his face. "She'd found the original plans for the house and property."

"Did you tell anyone about this?"

"No, but she'd left an entry—actually a reminder to herself—in her diary to tell Irmajean about the maze."

Irmajean, knowing eavesdropper's rarely hear anything good about themselves, held her breath. Was she about to learn something invaluable?

"And?"

"And Irmajean was naturally curious. You know how she is."

Barron grimaced. "Indeed I do."

"She can't believe I don't remember whether or not a maze existed. According to her, I've been here forever. She makes me feel like a fossil."

"And what did you tell her?"

"I try not to tell her anything—even though she's the most persistent busybody."

Irmajean waited a few moments more and decided she'd learned all she was going to. Besides, how long could she keep her presence unknown? She eased the back door open and was slipping out when she heard Ted say, "I wish the past would stay buried." That comment didn't startle her as much as bumping into Karl Webster. "You startled me. I thought you'd gone."

"I kinda got to worrying about you, so I came back. Interesting bit of conversation."

Irmajean thought interesting was an understatement.

Five

Irmajean had plenty of time to think about the things she'd overheard and to rationalize her own behavior. Wasn't anything permissible if it answered the question why Priscilla was murdered?

Her sweet husband met her at the back door. He took one look at her and asked. "What's the matter?"

"I think this might be the worst day of my life." And she threw her arms around him, giving him a tight hug. Then she went to sit on the cushiony sofa by the wood stove. There hadn't been a fire in it for over a month, but nonetheless it was psychologically warming. "I'm not sure anything will ever be all right again."

He sat next to her and took hold of her hand. "What happened? Have you had some kind of accident? What?" His voice, always calm, never betrayed what he was feeling.

She looked directly at him and with a great deal of effort kept her voice from breaking. "Priscilla's dead." Then before he could ask how, she added, "Murdered."

He said nothing for a moment. "You're not serious?"

Glancing down, she was surprised to find a calico cat purring in her lap. Stroking the soft fur provided a degree of normalcy and comfort. "I found her..." And she went on to explain. It was almost as disturbing to relate as it was to experience.

After a few quiet moments, he patted her hand and stood up. "Not to trivialize things, but I think you'll feel better if you have a cup of tea and some dinner." And he started toward the kitchen.

"I don't think I could eat a thing."

"You have to, Irmajean. Just a sandwich and a cup of tea."

Later when she'd finished her meal, her husband asked, "Now, don't you feel better?"

"At least the hollow feeling in my stomach is gone if not the one in my chest. Now I have a couple of calls to make. Frank wanted me to get the board members together for a meeting tomorrow, and I had to leave messages for a couple of them. So I think I'll try ringing them again."

When she reached Jim Mills, the high school history teacher, she almost wished she hadn't.

"I can't get off work at this late hour."

"And what would you do if you woke up sick tomorrow morning." She was too tired and upset to be diplomatic.

"I'd call in sick."

"Then if they could find a substitute on that short of a notice they can certainly find one if you call your principal tonight."

"Irmajean, I really don't appreciate this."

"And I don't appreciate you arguing with me after the day I've had. And especially after I told you this was a command appearance requested by the Chief of Police. In other words, attendance isn't exactly optional. I'll see you in the morning." Giving him no further chance to argue she hung up. What a pill that man could be.

Now she only had to call Rose Campion, a name she'd always felt had to be assumed. Lots of women bore the names of flowers, but for both the first and last names to qualify struck Irmajean as contrived. But then, what did it matter? The name conjured up a pleasant image of old-fashioned deep pink flowers with dusty green leaves growing in forgotten gardens. Hardly the image one got of the woman calling herself Rose Campion.

As Irmajean listened to the phone ring, she thought how little she knew about Rose. The young woman seemed to have made herself up with her almost gaudy clothing, name and profession. And how in the world did she support herself reading Tarot cards and selling herbal concoctions in a town the size of Pirate's Cove?

Rose's phone was eventually answered, but again by a machine. "Greetings, fellow inhabitants of Gaia. My energy is needed elsewhere, but please leave me a message, and I promise to communicate with you in some way."

"Rose, this is Irmajean Lloyd again. I'm calling by request of Frank Mallory our Chief of Police. He would like the Rosewood Board of Directors to meet in the usual place tomorrow morning at nine o'clock sharp. Attendance is *not* optional."

Her task completed Irmajean hung up the phone and turned her attention to the calico cat glaring on her lap. "There, there, Emily. I'm not ignoring you." She opened a package of lemon wafers her husband had placed on the table and dunked one in her tea. Although she always doubted she could eat a thing, it was an unfortunate fact that trauma always made her hungry, along with most everything else. She then turned her attention to her husband who had settled himself comfortably with a book while he waited for her to finish her phone calls.

"I just don't see why anyone would want to harm Priscilla, let alone kill her. True she could be a trifle bossy, but not enough to get anyone that upset, I wouldn't think." Irmajean turned back to her cookie to discover most of it floating in her tea. "Drat." And she fished the soggy remains out with a spoon.

"I'm remembering our conversation of this morning, about Priscilla's determination to prove Clarice might have killed her husband."

"I remember." She pursed her lips into a frown. "You advised me to leave well enough alone."

He nodded.

"But, Honey, surely that was all so long ago. Why would digging into a past long dead get her killed? There are no heirs. Nobody but Ted and Barron were even around then. They were a few years older than Chalmers, but only in their early teens."

"They still might have something to hide. And as far as them being the only holdovers from that era, aren't you forgetting Millicent?"

She gave him an incredulous look. "Millicent is eighty plus, scared of her own shadow and, therefore, hardly likely to track Priscilla to the attic."

"Desperation can drive a person to abnormal feats."

She tried and failed to picture whisper thin Millicent Morgan bashing Priscilla over the head and then heaving her inside the wall and down the spiral staircase. "I simply can't see her in the part."

"Maybe not. I was only pointing out that nobody should be overlooked."

Irmajean knew he was right, and that at tomorrow's board meeting she would be studying everyone suspiciously. The location of Priscilla's death suggested a certain familiarity with Rosewood, and who was more familiar with the property than the board of directors?

"There's something else."

"What?" His tone was wary.

"I made a little detour on the way home to check on Ted. He was so distraught over finding Priscilla's vandalized car that I was worried about him and wanted to make sure he was okay."

"And?"

"And I ran into Karl Webster leaving the house. He told me to go on in. And I did, even though I saw Barron Lancaster's car there. I only went as far as the kitchen."

He waited, saying nothing.

"I overheard a slightly disturbing conversation that leads me to believe they're hiding something."

"Any idea what?"

"Something to do with when they were young. Something that still haunts them both. I just have to figure out if it has anything to do with Priscilla's death."

He eyed her with alarm. "What do you mean?"

"Exactly what I said. You don't think I intend leaving this for Frank to solve, do you?"

"I would certainly hope that's exactly what you intended doing."

She reached over and patted his hand. "Honey, don't be ridiculous. No one knows Rosewood better than me now that Priscilla's dead."

"Exactly, and remember what she knew probably got her killed."

"I'll be careful. I'll just go about my usual business, and no one will even know I'm snooping."

He shook his head and his expression suggested he knew the battle was lost. "May I remind you that you are not indestructible?"

~ * ~

Irmajean stared up into the darkness. She'd abandoned the bedside mystery she'd been reading and turned out the light, but sleep seemed to have taken a holiday. Only Glenn slept, gently snoring beside her, while her mind buzzed with the implications of what had happened at Rosewood. Things would never be the same at the old house. Never. Priscilla was gone, and Irmajean had lost a friend. There would be no more cups of tea and conversation with the vibrant young woman with a passion for old houses. Had that passion and curiosity gotten her killed?

There was no getting around it. Irmajean would have to do some thorough digging into Rosewood's past. Like everyone else on the Board of Directors, she knew the basics. A lack of curiosity kept the others satisfied with that, while respect for Chalmers privacy even in death had kept Irmajean content in the gardens and out of the archives. But Priscilla's death might have changed all that and might make it necessary to poke about in Rosewood's closets in search of skeletons and answers.

Rosewood had become a second home in which she'd invested quite a bit of time and energy. She wasn't the only volunteer gardener, but she was the only one who was there almost every day.

She felt Priscilla's death on a personal level. Tears pricked at the back of her eyes. The vibrant young woman had only been twenty-nine with so much life ahead of her. This should never have happened. Never. Regardless of the fact that Frank Mallory might not approve and Honey definitely wouldn't, she was going to do everything she could to see that Priscilla's killer was brought to justice.

Six

Irmajean, dressed in loose fitting denim pants and a garden shirt with rows of marching vegetables, left early for Rosewood. The board meeting was scheduled for nine o'clock, and she wanted to take a quick walk round the garden first. If a hedge maze had once been a part of the Rosewood gardens all evidence of it had either been eradicated or overgrown. And Irmajean's fertile imagination began to turn over possibilities as to why, much as she would turn over the garden soil. The reference to a maze in Priscilla's diary seemed almost sinister in conjunction with her murder. This possibility, along with her discovery of the hidden staircase raised the question of how many other rumored secrets at Rosewood really existed. And if they were meant to be kept secret, what evil might their discovery unleash? What an addition a hedge maze would make to the house and garden tours. And yet, the same question kept surfacing over again. Why—if one existed—had it been allowed to disappear?

Much of the garden was dappled with morning sunshine and shadows. It was easy to let her imagination have the upper hand and almost imagine she saw ghosts from long ago garden parties. Except for an occasional bird song all was quiet. Irmajean meandered through the Moon Garden, where all white plants reflected moonlight, through the Boxwood garden, which was more formal, to the Native Plant area that sprawled in natural exuberance. Evergreen huckleberry, salal, red-flowering current, and thimbleberries thrived. Here the grass was allowed to grow a little tall and wildflowers to poke their heads up where ever they wanted. This was the most relaxing nook in the garden, perhaps because it lived up to its name with only minimal care. As Irmajean strolled along, she scanned the grounds for anything that might suggest the one time location of a maze.

Movement caught her attention, and she glanced to her left and discovered Catkin keeping pace with her. He often supervised her work in the garden and seemed to enjoy her company. They strolled into the Rose Garden where roses grew in a boundless abundance that enchanted even the least gardening inclined of visitors. Hybrid teas rubbed thorns with sprawling *rosa rugosas* and climbers draped themselves languidly over arbors at either end of this garden room. Two June weddings were scheduled when the roses would be at their showiest. Would Priscilla's death change those plans? Irmajean certainly hoped not because she knew how hard Priscilla had worked in planning them. Local history said the original mistress of Rosewood, Rachel Carmichael, had held elaborate garden parties among her beloved roses. Which would have made it the perfect spot for a maze to delight and entertain any children in attendance as well as the young at heart.

Irmajean stood in the gazebo that was the center of the Rose Garden, turning slowly around. Shadows melted into shadows creating visual barriers. Beyond the cultivated borders nature had taken over. Alders, salal, some huckleberry tangled together and, of course, the almost unstoppable blackberries, but for the first time Irmajean questioned why there were no towering evergreens to flank this part of the property as there were elsewhere. And now that the possibility of a hedge maze had taken root, she wondered if the absence of stately old fir trees was significant.

Irmajean sat on a stone bench and considered the possibilities. An errant breeze stirred the bushes and sent a brief shower of rose petals onto the path. A pair of sparrows bathed in a nearby birdbath, and an industrious bee burrowed in first one blossom and then another to emerge wearing pollen pantaloons. Nature carried on, oblivious to the tragedy marring Rosewood's tranquility.

Irmajean glanced over her shoulder and stood up. Giving up on the location if not the idea of a maze for the moment, she turned back toward the house. She'd been alone in the gardens many times and it had never bothered her, but then Priscilla Norris had still been alive. Now the flowers seemed to whisper secrets they were loathe to share, and the light breeze carried a chill.

She could tell from the cars parked outside Rosewood that almost everyone had arrived. The only vehicle she didn't see was Rose Campion's hard-to-miss, pea soup colored Volkswagen van. There was always the possibility she might not have gotten Irmajean's message. She'd be on hand if she had, asking questions and giving the

impression she was mentally taking notes. Irmajean
wished she could put her finger on why Rose seemed to
be acting a part, and that the real person behind her Rose
Campion persona would jump out some day and gleefully
exclaim, "Fooled you!"

Tess Brock, a local realtor, was just getting out of her
car and managing to expose a generous amount of leg.
The way the sun glinted off her improbable blond hair
Irmajean surmised it had recently been done. You had to
admire forty-something Tess's efforts to keep time at bay.
Unlike Irmajean who definitely looked as if her sand had
shifted—and knew it.

"Irmajean, do you know what's behind this morning's
command performance? Did Priscilla maybe abscond with
the silver?"

Irmajean almost said, "Haven't you heard?" But caught
herself in time. Frank Mallory was hoping for the element
of surprise in announcing Priscilla's death. It looked like it
was holding, at least in the case of Tess, although Pirate's
Cove like any small town was a hard place to keep a
secret. "Since Barron Lancaster insists on keeping the
silver in a safety deposit box, it doesn't seem likely."

They entered the house together, chatter and the
inviting smell of fresh coffee, greeting them. A platter full
of assorted scones and sweet rolls held center stage in the
middle of the table, and Irmajean, knowing her will power
far exceeded her won't power, groaned inwardly.

Frederick Blumer who never seemed comfortable
except when he was working or out of doors, prowled the
scant available floor space at the back of the room. He
was a local carpenter who spent his spare time

constructing beautiful furniture and walking his dog. He was a man who kept to himself and at the most talkative of times had little to say. Therefore Irmajean had been surprised when he'd asked to serve on the board of directors. While his contribution was rarely of a verbal nature, his free gratis repairs at Rosewood were perfection themselves.

Ted Myers was seated next to him and next to Ted was Millicent Morgan. Millicent was a little wren of a woman. Old as the hills, fluttery and dithery, and yet, she had carved out a considerable career for herself writing swashbuckling romance novels that would have made a sailor blush.

Tess Brock settled in a vacant chair next to Millicent, poured herself a cup of coffee then helped herself to a cheese Danish. "You'd better have something earth shattering to impart, Chief, because I couldn't get anyone to cover for me at the office, and I might be missing a chance at a million dollar sale."

Irmajean almost winced at Tess's comment, but knew the aggressive realtor wouldn't even be embarrassed when she did learn why Frank had summoned them all to a meeting. Tess was brash and unflappable. With her, the bottom line was money.

Barron Lancaster sat next to Tess and raised an eyebrow at her comment. Hard telling what Ted might have told him after she ceased eavesdropping..

Jim Mills pouted in a chair next to Barron. Irmajean knew he and Priscilla had dated a few times, but she suspected the interest was more on his part than Priscilla's. He was forty-six with thinning hair and a developing paunch while Priscilla was twenty-nine and very attractive. Irmajean reminded herself that now Priscilla would be forever twenty-nine with no chance to grow old. Someone—maybe even someone in this room— had robbed her of that opportunity. They mustn't be allowed to get away with it.

Frank came over to her and Irmajean hastened to inform him. "Everyone is here with the exception of Rose Campion. I couldn't reach her and had to leave a message. Although she's rarely on time and could get here yet."

"As long as she can account for her whereabouts on Friday, we'll let her off the hook."

Irmajean glanced at her fellow board members and thought—not for the first time—that they were an eclectic lot. But then it wasn't a passion for each other that had brought them together but for Rosewood. "Do you want to open the meeting, Frank?"

He hesitated, once again gauging the crowd, trying to memorize everyone's mood so that he could compare it with reactions to the announcement he was about to make.

Irmajean settled herself on the only vacant chair, an uncompromisingly hard one. Without asking, Ted Myers pushed a mug of well-stewed tea in her direction while Tess grinned and passed her the rapidly depleting supply of sweet rolls. With an inward sigh at her own weakness, Irmajean helped herself to a lavishly frosted cinnamon bun. Perhaps an hour or two of vigorous weeding would counteract its effects. Then she remembered that she'd left the house without breakfast and felt instantly vindicated.

Frank Mallory cleared his throat and an immediate hush spilled over the room.

"I'm glad you could all make it this morning, and I hope this meeting didn't put too much of a strain on anyone." He never liked breaking bad news and took a swallow of lukewarm coffee to lubricate his dry mouth. "Yesterday the police department received a report Priscilla Norris hadn't been seen at her apartment since early last Friday and that, from all appearances, she hadn't been there. So I came out here and interviewed Ted and Irmajean since they were available. We put our heads together and tried to come up with an explanation for her absence, since she'd given no indication she wouldn't be around."

Irmajean let her attention wander the room. Everyone present seemed to be hanging on Frank's every word. No one seemed to be fidgeting or looking the least bit uncomfortable.

Millicent Morgan, her eighty-two years giving her seniority, still raised her hand before speaking. "What makes you think anything might have happened? Perhaps she simply went away for a few days."

Frank silently cursed the octogenarian romance writer's interruption, but knew it was a reasonable question. Especially since he was spinning out the truth. "Everybody seems to know how fond Priscilla was of her little dog. Well, it seems he had been without food or water or a trip outside for some time. Priscilla's landlady had seen them Friday morning in the tall grass behind the apartment building. Ted says Priscilla was still at Rosewood when he left around three o'clock on Friday. So our job was to decide where she might have gone."

There was a brief buzz of conversation until Frank rapped his knuckles on the table. "The story isn't ended folks." He hesitated, again gauging his audience. "Yesterday afternoon Irmajean found Priscilla's body in the attic." He let the impact of his words sink in.

Jim Mills jumped to his feet, and Irmajean saw that he was pale despite the drugstore tan he always sported. "What are you saying, Chief?"

Barron Lancaster cleared his throat and stood up. "Yes, I think we all want to know what's going on."

Irmajean shifted on her hard chair and wondered if Frank wouldn't have been wiser to tell everyone in the beginning that Priscilla had been murdered.

"Priscilla was murdered sometime late Friday."

The board members gasped as one. Irmajean honestly couldn't have said if anyone looked momentarily guilty or if the stunned looks they all wore were genuine.

"How?" Jim Mills demanded. "How did she die?"

"We just have a preliminary report from the medical examiner, but it would seem a single crushing blow to the side of her head did the deed. Then she was stuffed inside an attic wall."

Irmajean could foresee all sorts of questions, but they were forestalled by a shuffle of feet and a thud. Barron Lancaster pushed Millicent Morgan aside and knelt beside Ted Myers. Irmajean abandoned her uncomfortable chair and moved to open a window. It was stuffy and Ted, never the most robust of men, had succumbed to the nerves that never seemed far away. She discounted his response because he already knew of Priscilla's death. If Ted gave anything away, it was his lack of stamina. Of that she was almost positive. Barron Lancaster was loosening Ted's tie, and Millicent retrieved his glasses, which hung askew from one ear.

Frederick Blumer had gone in search of a glass of water, which he now passed to Barron. Several seconds and a series of sputters later, Ted revived. Barron got to his feet and confronted Frank Mallory. "Don't you think your purpose would have been better served by breaking this news to us individually? After all, several of us, Ted in particular, had grown quite close to Priscilla."

"I wanted to gauge everyone's reaction to the bad news. This is after all a murder investigation."

If possible, Barron's ramrod straight stance became a little straighter. "You surely don't suspect any of us."

Frank gave a hitch to his gun belt. "We found her stuffed within an attic wall that hid a staircase once leading to the ground floor. This suggests someone familiar with the property. Until I know differently, I suspect everyone."

"For God's sake, Mallory. We all knew Priscilla Norris."

"Yes, and victims are more often than not murdered by people they know and trust. You should know that better than anyone, Lancaster."

Irmajean noticed every eye in the room was focused on Frank, and you could have heard a pin drop. Did that mean that what he was reporting was news to everyone? Or was someone, their anger spent, honing their acting skills? "We found evidence earlier that she'd been searching through boxes of old memorabilia in the carriage house. So we're considering the possibility she might have found something that contributed to her death. If anyone has even the smallest idea or bit of information they think might be helpful, please speak up." He waited but no one came forward. "All right then, I know each of you has given up something important to be here this morning. In an effort to minimize any further inroads on your time, I'd like a brief interview with each of you before you leave."

The groans were audible and he held up his hand. "Please remember, people, that someone you knew and worked with—maybe even liked—has been murdered. Someone young with what should have been a long life ahead of her. And it's very likely that her death has something to do with Rosewood. The common interest that brings you all together."

Irmajean had said little but she'd kept her eyes open gauging, as she knew Frank was, the reaction of the people gathered in Rosewood's dining room. Had Frank noticed in the commotion over Ted's collapse that Frederick Blumer had slipped from the room after bringing Ted a glass of water? Blumer was a bear of a man with a luxurious black beard that always looked as if it had received a jolt of electricity. By rights, he should have stood out in any crowd, but he moved so stealthily and said so little, that given other distractions, few ever noticed his comings and goings. And Irmajean would have bet that she was the only one who knew he'd left the room. She'd seen him do it before at board meetings— disappear. He always turned up later, usually in the process of doing some minor repair on the house.

As unobtrusively as she could, Irmajean worked her way through the throng of indignant board members. People who were sorry about Priscilla, but protested they had places they needed to be and they knew nothing so there was no sense in Frank wasting time questioning them. Besides, they had unimpeachable alibis. Irmajean knew some of them would be easily tested. But what about the others? Was one of the people present a killer? At one time or another she'd been alone with each and every one of them. In the ordinary course of events, none of them seemed capable of murder. Assuming one of them *had* murdered Priscilla, what had happened to push them over the edge?

Seven

Irmajean curious as to Frederick's whereabouts, closed the kitchen door behind her, shutting out some of the babble from the dining room. Where had he gone? It wasn't unusual for Frederick to wander off. He did it all the time. Didn't he realize such behavior made him look guilty? Knowing Frederick, he wouldn't care.

He might look like a bear, but Irmajean had seen him gently lift his sweet dog in and out of his truck last winter when the dog had some ligaments replaced. No small feat since she had to weigh about a hundred and fifty pounds. And she'd seen him stroking the woodwork at Rosewood after making some skilled repair. As if he truly believed the house had feelings. She couldn't see him bashing Priscilla's head in and stuffing her inside the attic wall. And in the unlikelihood that he had done just that, he would have skillfully removed and then replaced the tongue and groove panels of the attic. He would never have left the mess she'd found. Not even to throw suspicion away from him.

She moved quickly to one of the lace-curtained windows overlooking the parking area. With relief, she saw that his pickup, *Blumer Fine Carpentry* stenciled on the doors, was still parked out there. She liked Frederick for all his quiet ways. Maybe because of the way he treated his dog. Maybe because his passion for the house matched hers for the gardens of Rosewood. Nevertheless, she wanted to know where he was and why he'd gone there.

He couldn't have gone to the attic. Frank had stationed a policeman at the foot of the stairs to insure no one disturbed the scene of the crime. Still, perhaps she'd better check just to make sure. Her heart beating a little more rapidly than usual, Irmajean reentered the dining room and managed to exit into the living room without being seen. Or so she thought. At least no one called attention to her or tried to stop her. From the living room, she went to the entry and climbed the stairs to the second floor, hurried down the hallway to the attic stairs and almost collided with the policeman on duty.

"Oh!"

"Can I help you, Ma'am?"

Ma'am? Toby Wilkins used to bag her groceries when he'd worked at the local grocery store. She was tempted to remind him of that fact and then decided against it. After all, he was on duty and she *was* attempting to invade a crime scene. "Did a man with a beard come this way?"

"No, you're the first visitor I've had, Mrs. Lloyd."

She turned away. "That's good." Then added, "At least I think so." Before he could question her further, Irmajean fled the scene. *Where could Frederick have gone?* There was always the possibility that he might simply have gone to the bathroom. But he'd been absent far too long for that. Besides, Rosewood's plumbing was antiquated and noisy so it was darn near impossible to hide a visit to that facility.

It seemed unlikely he'd retreated to the gardens. Frederick's reason for serving on the board of directors was his interest in the preservation and restoration of old houses. Being careful not to sound like a herd of elephants descending the stairs, she reached the oak paneled entryway and pondered where to look next. Perhaps Frederick had gone to the basement office. It was the only other place in the house he could be. The shortest route was through the dining room to the kitchen and down the back stairs. But Irmajean didn't think she should push her luck by going that way. Sooner or later someone would notice her comings and goings. It was a given that Frank wouldn't approve of her tailing Frederick.

Irmajean closed the front door behind her, descended the porch steps and hurried around the walkway to the basement office door which was locked. Well, what had she expected? Not to be daunted, she peered into each and every window, but saw no one. Frustrated, she turned her back on the house and saw the door to the carriage house stood ajar. *Oh, joy!* She didn't think of herself as a timid person, but the carriage house was scarcely inviting at the best of times. Poorly lit and crowded with the shrouded relics of the late *North Coast Explorer*, it provided ample places for someone to hide. Not that she thought for a minute Frederick would want to harm her. She was after all following him for his own good. He probably had no idea how suspicious his absence made him look.

Irmajean entered the carriage house, hesitating for a moment by the barely open door in order to give her eyes a chance to adjust to the gloom and herself the opportunity to listen for the sound of any movement, however slight. There was nothing. However, if Frederick were upstairs and happened to glance out the window when she was crossing from the house, he'd know she was there. And if he hoped to go undiscovered, he might even now be holding his breath. Just as she uncomfortably discovered she was doing.

Really, all this skulking about was ridiculous. She had nothing to fear from Frederick. At least not with Rosewood full of people and two of them policeman. With determination she marched to the foot of the stairs and called out. "Frederick! Frederick, are you up there?" It was then she heard footsteps, not from overhead but from somewhere off to her left. She spun about, putting a wall of the carriage house to her back and peering into the shadows. One of which was definitely coming closer.

"Mrs. Lloyd, should you be wandering around by yourself—considering the police chief's revelation about Priscilla?" The carpenter's voice always sounded a bit rusty, like he was just getting over a bad sore throat.

He never called her anything but Mrs. Lloyd, no matter how many times she implored him to call her Irmajean. "Probably not. But then neither should you. Your leaving the proceedings in the dining room might look a bit suspicious."

"I wanted to have a look at something, and Ted's performance gave me the opportunity to slip away."

"You think that's what it was then? A performance?"

"Oh, it was probably genuine enough. Even a blind man could tell that he's scared stiff."

"You think so?"

He walked past her to sit on the bottom step of the stairs. "I think he knows something. Maybe not something about Priscilla's murder but something about Rosewood. Something that may have led to her death or maybe just something he's afraid others might find out."

Frederick didn't often say much, but when he did— "That's a lot of somethings, Frederick." She was inclined to agree that Ted's panic was very real, but didn't say as much in the hopes Frederick might be more specific. She suspected that Frederick was a noticer, and he might have noticed something—that word again—she'd missed.

"Well, since I don't know what it could be..."

"Could you perhaps make a guess?" Irmajean was persistent.

He seemed to be searching for words. "I never met Chalmers Carmichael, but did he have anything in common with Meyers and Lancaster?"

"They were related through their grandparents."

"That might be why they'd get together for Christmas dinner, but once a week?" He leaned forward conspiratorially. "What'd they talk about all those times— a shyster lawyer, an old maid in pants, and a paper and ink gossip?"

Irmajean almost choked on an unbidden laugh at his apt descriptions. "You make those regular-as-clockwork lunches sound positively sinister."

"Mrs. Lloyd, you're a watcher, like me. You can't tell me you didn't ever wonder what secret they have in common."

Irmajean was conscious even in the dusky lighting of the carriage house that while she was pumping Frederick for information he was doing the same to her.

"You know Mrs. Lloyd, few people really know this old place."

"Priscilla was trying..."

He looked down at his hands, knotted together into one huge fist. "She was looking to open old wounds."

"I don't think she saw it that way."

"Maybe she should have. Maybe then, she'd still be alive. Some secrets are best left alone."

It was an eerie echo of her husband's warning yesterday morning—a lifetime ago.

"And how are we to identify which secrets should be kept and which revealed?"

"Listen to the house, to the property the way you listen to the garden. I've watched you sitting there on one of the benches I built, your eyes closed, listening. People don't look outside themselves or pay attention to what their surroundings are telling them."

"So, Frederick, do you think you understand Rosewood's secrets?"

"I was out here that one day last winter when we got a little snow. Which gave me a rare opportunity to observe something interesting. You didn't happen to be out here that day did you?"

"No, the roads were slick. Remember we cancelled a board meeting because of it."

"Too bad, because I bet you would have noticed."

"Noticed what, Frederick?" Honestly, was the man being deliberately cryptic?

"That the snow didn't stick in certain places. That there was a path from the house and into the gardens where the snow didn't stick at all."

"You're losing me, Frederick."

"Before I moved here, I worked at a college back East as their head carpenter. A private school situated on the grounds of an old estate. When it snowed, there were paths through the snow where it didn't stick. Rumor had it there were underground passages connecting the main house with other buildings on the property."

"And so you think there might be an underground passage here at Rosewood?" She made no effort to keep the excitement from her voice. This was the first she'd heard of such a thing on the property.

"Maybe..."

"Why then haven't we ever found any access to it?"

"For the same reason we've never found any trace of the other things rumored to have once existed at Rosewood. Somebody took care to hide them. Don't you wonder why Ted Meyers is in such a panic that he's fainting?"

"I don't think Ted has what it takes to kill someone."

"Don't kid yourself, Mrs. Lloyd. Everyone has what it takes to kill given enough provocation." He got to his feet causing Irmajean to step backward and bump into the wall. He passed her walking toward the door when the carriage house door swung wide.

Ted Myers, seemingly recovered, stood there peering at them. "There you are. I've been looking for you, Frederick. Chief Mallory wants a word with you."

Irmajean watched the nervous little man follow Blumer back to the house not noticing her in the least and leaving her with the impression that she might be invisible. When she returned to Rosewood, she saw that everyone with the exception of Barron Lancaster had left. Was he hanging around for some reason or was he still to be questioned? Irmajean didn't much care for him, and it always took every effort at good manners not to show it. For his part, he frequently gave her the impression that she vaguely amused him. A feeling she didn't care for at all. The only thing they had in common was their interest in Rosewood.

Barron crossed one leg over the other, being extremely careful not to disturb the crease in his pants. As she watched him, Irmajean reflected that she'd never seen him in anything other than a suit. Perhaps even his pajamas were cut in the same tailored style.

"Well, Irmajean, what have you been up to while the rest of us came under the keen scrutiny of Chief Mallory?"

Lancaster's knowing expression suggested she wasn't fooling him a bit. "It *was* a bit stuffy in here, what with all the righteous indignation and declarations of innocence. What about you, Irmajean? Where were you last Friday?"

"I've already accounted for my whereabouts to the police, thank you." She owed him nothing.

"Interesting how circumspect we would all be if we knew we might be called to account for every second of our time."

"Not a world I'd care to be a part of, thank you. And you, Barron, where were you on Friday?" She glanced at his gently swinging foot and saw that the sock on his right leg was a bit wrinkled. It was quite a cheering observation.

"Alas, I was driving back from Portland. Alone and unrecognized by anyone I passed. The only thing to speak for me is my known character."

And that, she thought, *should be enough to put you in the soup.* Aloud she said, "We certainly are all well acquainted with that, aren't we?" Then she turned around to hide the smile that followed his quick frown.

Thankfully, the door to the kitchen opened and Frank Mallory emerged. "Did Ted leave?" Frank directed his question at Barron.

"I believe he went downstairs to the office."

"Damn! I don't want anybody messing around in there." The police chief stomped off to return in a matter of minutes with Ted Myers in tow. "I'm through with everyone, with the exception of you, Irmajean. So Ted and Barron, you can go now."

Ted opened and closed his mouth several times in an unintentional parody of a fish gasping for air. "I really have work to do. Things that didn't get done yesterday."

"They're going to have to wait a while longer, Ted. I'll let you know when you can come back to work."

Barron came to Ted's aid. "Really, Chief, is this necessary? The running of Rosewood needs to go on regardless."

Frank Mallory heaved a sigh that must have given a clue to his frayed patience. "I'm not shutting Rosewood down, just putting it on hold for a couple of days. Then Ted can get on with doing all the things he does to keep this place up and running."

Ted's fussy hand-fluttering and Barron's frown indicated their lack of enthusiasm for abandoning Rosewood, but Frank had made it clear they really didn't have any other choice. It wasn't often that Barron Lancaster was the one railroaded rather than the other way around and Irmajean fought to hide her amusement. Once they were out the door, Frank turned to her. "Irmajean, I'd like you to do me a favor, if you will."

"I'll certainly try."

"Will you go through everything in Priscilla's office and see if you can come up with *anything* that seems out of place or unusual? You know what's been going on at Rosewood. What programs are in the planning stage. Who's in charge of what and who's volunteered. I keep thinking the answer to who killed her might be staring us right in the face if we only knew where to look. I'm ninety-nine percent sure it has something to do with Rosewood. With something that was going on here or might have gone on in the past." He gave Irmajean a knowing look. "It hasn't escaped my notice that Ted's tail is in a knot over something. He's scared and not doing a very good job of hiding it. But scared as he is, he's not giving anything away. That tells me he's more frightened of whatever it is he's hiding than he is of getting in trouble with me for withholding evidence." Frank gave a hitch to his gun belt. "Too often in my experience, no one tells the whole story. Not even someone as truthful as you, Irmajean."

What did he think she was keeping from him?

Her puzzlement must have shown, because he sought to explain. "When are you going to tell me why you slipped out of the house, and what you were doing in the carriage house with one of the suspects? You didn't think Ted would keep that to himself did you?"

"Surely you don't seriously suspect Frederick Blumer?"

"I'm suspicious of everyone at this point. So, are you going to tell me what you were doing? What he was doing?"

She jammed her hands into the deep pockets of her garden shirt, her fingers closing around a roll of twine and a pair of clippers. "There's not that much to tell. I noticed that Frederick had left the room. It's something he does frequently during board meetings. I don't know if he gets restless, bored or if maybe he's a bit claustrophobic. I wondered where he'd gone. Thinking perhaps he didn't realize how bad it looked for him to just up and leave during a police investigation. I found him in the carriage house." She hesitated for a moment realizing she didn't know for certain what he'd been doing in the carriage house. His tale of an underground passage might just have been a red herring.

"And did he tell you why he was there?"

"We talked of other things."

Frank waited expectantly.

"He thinks Priscilla's snooping got her killed."

"Now isn't that an original thought?"

Irmajean ignored the police chief's sarcasm. "He also thinks Ted and Barron are hiding something.'

"Yeah, well, tell me something I don't know." He ran his hand through his thinning hair. "Nobody claims to know anything. The worst of it is, I pretty much believe they're telling the truth."

Her relief coupled with disappointment. She didn't want to think anyone she knew was guilty of murder. Yet was it likely Priscilla would have invited a stranger to see what she'd found in the attic?

"Irmajean, can you get right on going over the office? See if there's anything that doesn't fit.'

Her spirits rose. He was giving her permission to snoop. Not that she wouldn't have anyway. But it was nice to know doing so wouldn't get her in trouble with the police. She tried to keep her tone casual. "Sure, I'll have a look around."

Irmajean locked all the access doors to the office as soon as Chief Mallory left. She wasn't particularly concerned about being alone in the house. Her volunteer hours at the property had it feeling like a second home. But she didn't want to be looking over her shoulder at every sound. Rubbing her hands together, she looked around the office. Where to begin? First of all she'd call her husband and let him know what she was up to. The basement of Rosewood was an interesting place. The outside facing of the foundation was covered in stone and windows were placed at regular intervals the entire circumference. This was no dark hidey hole for storing and forgetting junk. There was a utility corner with washer and dryer and a small bathroom. Otherwise, the basement was a well organized office. This was due in part to Priscilla and in part to Ted. She felt a little guilty preempting what they both thought of as his domain. She knew how she would feel if she was banned from the garden while Ted was given free rein. Well, it couldn't be helped. She was on an official mission and the sooner she started the sooner she could finish up. And the sooner Ted could have his office back.

Priscilla's desk seemed the logical place to begin. Unfortunately she didn't discover much, except that Priscilla was fond of leaving notes to herself saying do this and do that and look here for this and there for that.

There was also a note saying, *Pick up food for Catkin.* Which reminded Irmajean that she hadn't seen the wily beast all morning. He liked people and was usually around for any and all meetings, trying out the various laps of those present. Unless he'd put in an appearance while she was holding her *tête á tête* with Frederick Blumer, he was conspicuously absent. Oh well, it was a fine day outside, and he was probably monitoring the bird population in the garden. She would remember to put food out for him before she left. But Catkin's hold on her thoughts was soon superseded by a file she found wedged in the back of the top desk drawer.

Interestingly enough the folder contained photocopies of various newspaper articles, all of them having to do with Rosewood and reaching well into the past. Priscilla had been doing her homework. Irmajean cleared a place on Priscilla's desk and began looking through the collection of photocopied clippings.

Rosewood had indeed been the center of social activities. Chalmers mother had hosted an annual charity tea that was even mentioned in the Portland papers.

Grainy pictures showed elegantly dressed women wearing big picture hats and holding fragile looking teacups, and much was made of the lavish display of roses. But what interested Irmajean the most was a single line near the end of one particular article.

Children and the young at heart delight in exploring the hedge maze modeled after the famous Hampton Court Maze in England. It is an accurate replica even to size, approximately a quarter of an acre. While not terribly complicated it is nevertheless a great source of merriment for young and old alike. Someone, she would presume Priscilla, had highlighted these few lines with yellow highlighter and written in the margin, *Important!!*

Irmajean relaxed against the back of the chair. This must have been what prompted the memo in Priscilla's date book. A discovery the late director must have made while Irmajean was gone. Here was proof in black and white that a hedge maze had once existed on the property. A topiary endeavor that no one claimed to know anything about. Now why was that? Barron and Ted were both over seventy, so even if it had been abandoned when they were children they couldn't be ignorant of it. So why did they pretend to be? And why would something as much of an undertaking as a replica of the Hampton Court Maze be allowed to return to nature? She was mulling this over without success when someone startled her by tapping on the frosted glass panel of the door.

Eight

Karl Webster nursed his ailing truck up the driveway with the hope he could get to his camp before the aged vehicle gave out. As it sputtered and crept past Teddy's place, Karl noticed that his benefactor wasn't at home. Then he remembered that it was Tuesday and every Tuesday Teddy had lunch with Barron Lancaster. This was also the day Teddy ran all of his errands. Karl knew from experience that you could set your watch by the old guy's habits. Which meant nobody would be at home for awhile.

With a sharp turn of the wheel, Karl brought his truck around by the garage and listened to it sputter and die. He'd have to hope it would start up after a rest. Meanwhile, he'd help himself to Teddy's groceries and maybe have a snoop around. He'd always respected Teddy's privacy, after all the old guy couldn't have too many secrets, but the bits and pieces of conversation he'd overheard the night before had gotten him to wondering just how many skeletons *were* cluttering up old Teddy's closets.

Given the way morals and public opinion about what was scandalous and what wasn't had changed in the last twenty years, maybe their secret wasn't much to get excited about. And then again, maybe it was. Personally, he didn't care what Teddy might have done just so long as the old guy didn't take an axe to him some night. Webster chuckled to himself at the picture that conjured up. Still, sometimes the most unlikely people did the most bizarre things. That is if you could believe the tabloids and trash TV.

Webster let himself into the house, calling out just in case. He wanted to make sure Teddy hadn't broken with old habits. While Teddy was used to him walking right on in, it wouldn't do to have his little buddy catch him actually snooping. His only response was silence. Karl closed the door behind him and decided where to begin. He'd never been upstairs, but then even Teddy rarely went up there any more, preferring to confine his housekeeping—such as it was—to the main floor. Even the basement door hadn't been unlocked in years. Teddy even claimed the key was lost. Was the thing that had Teddy so jumpy down there? Or had the old guy simply decided he didn't need as much house as he had? The logical thing would have been to sell out and get an apartment in town. But Karl knew Teddy would never consider that, even if the house fell down around his ears. A small apartment in town would have absolutely no prestige. Not that Karl thought a tumble down ruin in the country much better, but he knew it made all the difference to Teddy. He knew first hand how important family was to the old guy.

He decided to have a look upstairs. The treads were narrow, the stairwell poorly lit, and the carpet worn. But he knew nothing had been replaced since Teddy's mother had died. Not even the kitchen stove, now with only one burner that worked. What an odd, uneventful life Teddy had led, or so Karl had assumed until the conversation he'd overheard last night. Now it seemed likely that the old guy had taken part in something so horrifying that years later he was still shaking in his boots. Whatever it was, he feared Priscilla Norris's murder would bring it to light. Karl was fond of his reluctant landlord and in his own way looked out for him. He sure as heck hoped Teddy wasn't involved in Priscilla's murder, but just in case, Karl felt justified in having a snoop around the family homestead.

Four good-sized bedrooms occupied the second floor, all of them dark and over-furnished. Heavy draperies covered every window, so Karl had no qualms about switching on lights. The damp, dusty, silent rooms illuminated, it was difficult deciding where to begin looking. Especially since he hadn't a clue what he was looking for. Just something Teddy might consider shameful or scandalous. And that was darn near everything except the air he breathed.

Closets were full of hatboxes and out of style clothing and the bureaus were so crammed Karl could hardly get the drawers closed once he got them open. Ten minutes into his search and he could see that a thorough investigation would require one of the days when Teddy volunteered at Rosewood. In fact, it would probably take him a whole day for each room. Why in the world did Teddy keep all this old crap? But then Karl was a minimalist. If it didn't fit in the back of his decrepit truck, then he didn't need it.

Karl had exited the last bedroom and headed toward the stairs when he noticed a heavy cord dangling from the ceiling. He had to jump up in order to reach it, but once in hand he gave it a tug then stepped quickly out of the way as a pull down stairway descended with a shower of dust. Grit was everywhere, including his eyes and throat. After a coughing fit that left him seeing stars, he realized here was easy access to the attic. Webster knew he wouldn't have long to poke around, but it was hard to resist the temptation provided by those stairs.

He climbed them cautiously, since he'd never make a getaway if he fell and broke a leg. They creaked beneath him, but seemed up to his weight. He stuck his head through the opening, breaking through decades of cobwebs. Brushing them away from his face, he climbed into the attic, searched for and found the string to a light that still worked.

At a glance, he saw the expected boxes, trunks and miscellaneous accumulation of a century. Stuff to be stored in the attic and saved for a time that hadn't come yet or maybe had passed unnoticed. He was crouched low, looking under the eaves when a fully clothed dressmaker's dummy gave him a start. For an uncomfortable fraction of a second, until he recognized it for what it was, he thought that he'd been caught. The sigh of relief that followed didn't last long. For when he went to move out of the dummy's corner he noticed something even more peculiar under one of the windows allowing scant light into the attic. It looked like someone stretched out asleep on a narrow cot.

Karl crept towards it, action motivated by the unlikeliness of what he thought he saw. There couldn't be anybody asleep up here. Not with all the dust that had rained down on him when he'd opened the stairs. So what was he seeing? Possibly something as easily explained as the dressmaker's dummy. In reality, something so unexpected as to be unbelievable. Karl reached out a hand to touch the thing and prove what he was seeing was real, but jerked his fingers away in revulsion. He couldn't do it, couldn't touch it. More than likely this was what had Teddy in a twit. And for good reason. There, where it must have rested for years if dust and cobwebs were any indication, was a corpse.

"Geez, Teddy." Karl muttered as he stared fascinated at what had once been a man. Or so he would assume until he knew better. Skeletal arms rested across the chest and bones were visible through holes in tattered clothing. Karl shook his head in disbelief. This had to be the secret

Teddy lived with day in and day out. A dusty, battered carpetbag was shoved under the cot and Karl reached to dislodge it in the hopes he might learn who this had once been. His search of the contents turned up a pathetic array of once treasured belongings.

"Don't!"

Karl jumped up, cracking his head on a rafter.

"Don't disturb his rest—please."

Karl rubbed at a spot he suspected would be tender tomorrow. "I didn't hear you come in..." Lame but true.

"Why did you come upstairs? Up here? Is this the first time or have you regularly abused my hospitality?"

Karl reflected that Teddy had learned something from years of associating with Barron Lancaster. He'd neatly turned the tables on Karl, focusing on the fact the younger man was trespassing rather than on an explanation of why he had a body stashed in his attic. Karl wasn't about to be so easily routed. 'Who is he, Teddy? And what's he doing in your attic? Wouldn't a decent burial have been preferable?" Except Karl knew a decent burial would have called attention to the fact this man was dead. And left as he'd been to decompose in Teddy's attic, Karl would bet attention was the last thing wanted.

Ted moved toward him. "Why did you have to go snooping around? I thought I could trust you." His voice rose, accusing, angry.

For the first time since meeting Teddy, Karl felt almost afraid. At the very least, apprehensive. There was anger in the old guy's eyes and a cold edge to his accusation. If the body on the cot was any indication, maybe old Teddy wasn't as harmless as he looked.

"Look, I can keep my mouth shut. This guy's been history for a long time. Why should I blab to anybody?"

"You mustn't let anybody know he's here."

Karl couldn't help asking. "Why is he here?"

Ted had reached his side and looked down at the earthly remains resting on the cot. "He was such a nice man. He didn't deserve what happened to him."

Karl took a couple of steps backward, away from Teddy and closer to escape. Still, he wanted to know, "And what was that?"

"I suppose you could say he was scared to death."

Not much of an answer. "Who was he, Teddy?"

"Rosewood's shame."

Nine

Once she resumed breathing normally, Irmajean was able to recognize the distorted image of her husband through the frosted glass of the door. "Really," she muttered to herself. "Who did you think might be standing there?" She was uncomfortably aware of the answer. No amount of assumed bravado changed the fact she was alone in a house where a murder had occurred recently. And the victim—despite the years separating them in age—had been a good friend.

Unlocking the door, Irmajean meant to scold Glenn for giving her a start. But when she saw he was holding their well-traveled picnic basket, she didn't have the heart. Especially when he announced after crossing the threshold, "I brought lunch."

She was more than a little suspicious that lunch was an excuse to check on her, and she decided not to scold him for giving her a fright. "It's good to see you—and lunch. But I thought you were headed north."

"I put that off until tomorrow."

"I can make us some tea or instant coffee. Which would you prefer?"

He pulled up a chair to the side of the desk and began unloading the lunch he'd brought. "I'd prefer that you not be out here by yourself until they catch Priscilla's killer. I've got stacks of work to do, and I certainly can't do it if I'm worrying about you. I'm not too happy with Frank Mallory for asking you to stay and go through Priscilla's office."

Irmajean patted her husband's hand. "I don't think he would have suggested it if he'd thought I'd be in any kind of danger. Besides, as you can see, I've locked myself in."

"But are you positive you're alone in the house?"

She gave him a startled look.

He peered at her over his glasses. "I brought some work with me. I'll keep out of your way, but you're not staying out here by yourself."

She was touched by his thoughtfulness but not surprised. She didn't question the relief she felt. "What did you bring us for lunch?"

"Tuna on rye and a 7Up a piece. And some of those good ginger cookies from the bakery." He took a generous bite of sandwich, chewed thoughtfully, swallowed and then asked with a hopeful tone, "Have you found anything useful?"

"I don't know about useful, but certainly interesting." She passed him the folder Priscilla had filled with photocopies of newspaper articles concerning Rosewood. "I know a thing or two about plants and I've done my very best to identify and restore the gardens here. But I've accomplished what I have in a hands-on manner. Trimming away brush and grass from around existing plants, pulling weeds. Much of what I've done has been salvage work. I never questioned the absence of any written records concerning the garden—always intended to dig a little deeper and see if I could find any." She took a bite of sandwich, "If I had, I might have discovered there *was* at one time a hedge maze here at Rosewood." She tapped the file of newspaper clippings. "I feel I've somehow betrayed the vision of Rachel Carmichael and Rosewood. The gardens were—are glorious, but to locate and restore the hedge maze would really put the property on the social register of historic houses in this country. And if we're going to find the funding to continue, I'm afraid it might take just that kind of a miracle."

While his wife chatted, Glenn read through the articles she'd indicated. "This is interesting, but certainly no reason for you to feel you've let the gardens down. Or Rachel Carmichael. None at all. If it weren't for you, the gardens would still be a hopeless tangle—like mats on a woolly dog. Now you know there's a hedge maze you can throw your energies into rescuing it."

Irmajean rested her chin on her clasped hands. "Why do you suppose it wasn't kept up? And what's even stranger is that no one connected with the property has ever mentioned it. Why? Rosewood was like a second home to Ted and Barron. And Millicent has lived in Pirate's Cove forever. It's almost like there was a conspiracy of silence."

"Irmajean, don't you think you might be reaching a bit? You know what condition the gardens were in when Chalmers died. Yet no one thought that was strange or sinister. People knew he didn't have the money or the inclination or maybe both, to keep them up. If pulling a few weeds was beyond him then, how can you expect him to have maintained anything as elaborate as a hedge maze? Remember, gardens aren't as important to everyone as they are to you."

"Honey," and her voice rose as she climbed up on her verbal soap box, "this is not a variety of tulip we're talking about. This is a major architectural garden design that seems to have conveniently slipped everybody's mind. And tell me why Priscilla was murdered shortly after she discovered evidence of the maze?"

"That might just be coincidence." Glenn thought for a moment while finishing his sandwich. "We talk about Chalmers, Ted and Barron as if they were ancient. Chalmers was only in his sixties when he passed away. The other two are in their early seventies. This house is a hundred years plus. That maze could very well have been neglected long before any of them came along. Check the dates on these articles. Not a one of them is any more recent than the mid nineteen-twenties. You know how quickly a garden can become overgrown when it's neglected."

Irmajean clung tenaciously to her suspicions. "I think Ted and Barron know everything there is to know about this property as well as their own. So what's keeping them quiet on the subject of the maze? What's the big secret?"

Honey heaved a very heavy sigh. "Now that you have proof one existed, why don't you ask them? Personally, I don't think Ted could stop fussing long enough to murder anyone and Lancaster is too fastidious and well-pressed."

Irmajean fired her husband an amazed look. "I don't think Frank would consider a crease in somebody's trousers as much of an alibi." She heaved a heavy sigh. "The answer must be here somewhere."

"Have you looked everywhere in the office?"

"Not yet."

"I can spare an hour or two so why don't I help you look."

Irmajean looked at the armload of work he'd brought with him. "Are you sure about that?"

He glanced meaningfully around the room lined with filing cabinets. "Unless you want to be stuck in here rather than out in the garden, I think somebody has to help."

Irmajean glanced ruefully out the window at the sunlight warming the grounds. There was so much work to be done and only a handful of volunteers to accomplish it. And she was the only one who could be there every day. "Frank does want me to have a look for anything I think might be unusual or out of place. Perhaps as a reward to ourselves after several hours of diligent searching, we could take a stroll around the gardens, particularly the tea garden."

"I suppose you'll be wanting to take a pair of clippers."

"Well, there's always something that needs pruned." She patted her pocket, reminding her husband of the earthworm she'd deposited there once for safekeeping and then forgotten. It had crawled out and landed in his slipper to be discovered only in the middle of the night. Needless to say, safekeeping was no longer a part of that worm's vocabulary.

Glenn took one side of the room and Irmajean the other. "Don't let me forget to take the mail that's been left in the mail basket. Ted was too flustered yesterday to think of it, and I don't know how soon Frank will let him back in here."

"Okay."

After sorting through a number of filing cabinets, Irmajean straightened and rubbed her aching back. "We've been at this for two hours. We not only deserve a break but I need one."

"I hope you didn't need the rest of your sandwich."

"I only left a couple of bites..." Then she saw what he meant. Catkin perched big-as-you-please on the desk and the minute piece of lettuce dangling from his mouth indicated he had enjoyed the remains of her tuna fish sandwich. "Now where did *he* come from?"

"What do you mean where did he come from? I was under the impression he lived here."

Irmajean waved this aside. "No, no, that's not what I meant. Of course he lives here. But I haven't seen him all day and was beginning to wonder if something had happened to him. Like getting shut in somewhere, although he does appear in the most unlikely places at the most unexpected times. It makes me wonder..."

"Makes you wonder what?"

"If he knows about entrances and exits that we don't."

Glenn crumpled up the wax paper he'd used to wrap the tuna sandwiches. "He's a cat. Of course he does."

"Well, if this cat wasn't so darned secretive he might be able to answer a lot of questions. Like where he's been all morning and how he got in here."

"He's undoubtedly been asleep, keeping his own counsel until he smelled the tuna fish. Hope of a snack brought him out of hiding."

"But why didn't one of us see him while searching the office?"

"Because he didn't want us to."

"Honestly, Honey, you talk like there's something supernatural about him."

"You've said more than once you thought he could walk through walls."

"I was speaking metaphorically."

"Whatever, you're metaphor is getting ready to walk away. Why not follow him and see where he goes?"

With a loud thud, Catkin landed on the floor. He paused, inspected his back leg and groomed his tail. Then with a twitch of said appendage he slipped behind the nearest filing cabinet.

"Quickly! Follow him."

Honey glanced at his wife and then back at the narrow space the cat had squeezed into. Irmajean glared at him and said. "You know what I mean. I don't want him to get away without knowing where he goes. Between the two of us we can surely move those filing cabinets."

"Irmajean, they're metal and they're full."

"Then we'll unload them, but I want to know where Catkin disappears." She was down on her hands and knees peering behind the file cabinet. "There's something back there." And she indicated the filing cabinet. "Help me move it."

Knowing a losing battle when he saw one, Glenn moved around to the opposite side of the cabinet, which budged only reluctantly, but enough for Irmajean to gain a better look.

She rocked back on her heels. "You won't believe it!"

"Try me."

"There's an opening in the wall just large enough for a cat." She struggled to her feet with some help from her husband. "Let's unload the file cabinet so we can pull it completely away from the wall."

It only took a few minutes to methodically remove the files in the cabinet. That done, the piece of furniture moved easily. Irmajean pointed triumphantly. "What did I tell you?"

'It's a heating vent. Has to be, but somebody's removed the cover. What kind of heat did there used to be in the house before an oil furnace was put in? Do you know?"

"There was a wood burning furnace, but Chalmers replaced it years ago. Maybe he left the vent off for Catkin to wander."

"That doesn't seem likely."

"Well, maybe not, but do you realize what this probably means?"

"No, but I'm sure you'll tell me."

"If the cover is off the vent here in the basement and Catkin comes and goes, then there must be another uncovered vent somewhere."

Glenn nodded. "Probably. But does that solve anything."

She looked a bit crestfallen then perked up. "It answers the question of how Catkin often gets from place to place."

"With that mystery solved, let's put these files back and go home."

"But I haven't found what I was looking for."

"There's always tomorrow."

She knew he was right. "Then what about our walk around the garden?"

Glenn checked his watch. "Have you forgotten that we're due at the Mallory's for bridge tonight?"

"I had, yes. I guess we'd better forego our stroll. Maybe Frank will have something to tell us."

"There may not be anything he can tell us."

Irmajean knew he was trying to discourage her from becoming too involved in the investigation, but she couldn't help having an interest. After all, Rosewood and a good friend were involved. "Let's go out through the front door. That way I can make certain everything is locked up."

Glenn trailed dutifully behind, bumping into his wife when she stopped suddenly in the middle of the upstairs foyer. "Oooph! You might signal when you plan on making an abrupt stop."

"Sh-h-h! Do you hear that?" And she held her hand up to silence him.

He strained to hear, not so much because he wanted to, but because he didn't want to disappoint Irmajean. And his efforts paid off. There was a sound coming from inside the paneled wall. "Mice? It must be."

Irmajean approached the panels, trying to track the sound they heard and in so doing tipped over a tall basket filled with Pampas Grass. Miniscule pieces of the grass flew everywhere and she righted the container before turning to rap sharply on the wall. There was a response they would have missed if they hadn't been listening intently. "Catkin, is that you?" There was an answering meow.

She took a hold of her husband's arm and shook it gently. "If there's room for Catkin then there's more than the usual space within those walls. Don't you see what's beginning to surface?" Without giving him a chance to respond she continued on. "There have long been rumors about secret places at Rosewood. The places exist; Priscilla discovered that to her misfortune. Ted's about ready to jump out of his skin and Barron won't leave him alone if he can help it. Which indicates—I think—that Ted knows something and Barron is afraid he'll tell it."

"And you think it's connected with Priscilla's murder."

"Now that Chalmers is gone, who knows this house better than they do? Walled up staircases, hidden rooms, underground tunnels—they're all just conjecture for most of us. But Ted and Barron would know for certain. Yet they've said nothing. Then Priscilla is found murdered, her body stuffed inside the walls of the attic. What else do they find inside that wall? A boarded up staircase. I think Ted and Barron knew of its existence. You should have seen Ted after he discovered Priscilla's car. He was not only upset but terrified."

"What about Barron? Can you exonerate him as well?"

"He claims to have been on his way home from the city. I imagine he was somewhere at sometime that would provide him with an alibi."

Glenn shrugged. "The only person I know couldn't have done it, is you." He reached over to brush at her shoulder. "You're covered with feathery bits of Pampas Grass."

She looked down and frowned, knowing full well some of them were bound to end up in her dinner. "Honey, I'm not going to be happy until I know why all these secret places were built into the property and then why they were boarded up."

He gave a heavy sigh, but kept silent. Irmajean determined was not to be deterred. She rattled the door handle after closing the door behind them. "It's locked."

"It would seem so."

She was in the car and fastening her seat belt when she remembered something she'd intended to do but had forgotten. "I forgot the mail in the out basket."

"It isn't going anywhere." Glenn wanted his dinner, not another diversion.

"True, but it's been there since Friday."

"And it will be there tomorrow." He started the engine and began backing away from the house. "Besides, we're too late anyway."

"Too late?"

"To make today's mail."

"You're right. Anyway what could there be in that mail basket that might shed some light on Priscilla's murder?"

Ten

"Two clubs."

Irmajean frowned when she heard her husband's opening bid. She and Glenn had walked over to Jane and Frank Mallory's for their bi-monthly bridge game. A get together she always looked forward to, but even more so this evening because she hoped that Frank would talk about the trouble at Rosewood. She knew from experience that often things were revealed during friendly chatter that might not be otherwise. However, he had stated as soon as they walked in the door that he wanted to put Rosewood on hold until they broke for dessert.

When the time came, Irmajean gazed with envy on the flaky piecrust. "Where did you get these Marionberries?"

"I had them in the freezer. Have to make room for this year's crop."

Irmajean supposed she should cook a little bit more and garden a little less. But daffodils never disappointed and soufflés often did.

Frank glanced up from his pie and directly at Irmajean. "I know you're bursting to talk about Rosewood. Find anything that might be helpful?"

"Not yet, although I did run across something that raises some interesting questions. Priscilla had accumulated a surprising amount of information on the history of the property. She really did give good value for the dollars we paid her. I'll miss her belief in Rosewood's potential—and her enthusiasm, which was so different from some of the curmudgeons on our board of directors."

Frank eyed her through the steam drifting up from his coffee. "More than one person interviewed mentioned you got along better with Priscilla than anyone else. To quote Millicent Morgan, the two of you were quite chummy."

Irmajean almost choked. "Only Millicent or perhaps Ted would use a word like that to describe our rapport. But yes, I got along quite well with Priscilla. Which wasn't surprising considering I have two daughters in the neighborhood of Priscilla's age."

"It was suggested Priscilla could be a bit pushy in getting what she wanted. Tess Brock compared her to a steamroller. Would it be safe to say she didn't get along with everyone?"

Irmajean thought for a minute before attempting to explain the complex relationship that existed between Priscilla and the board of directors. "The board hired Priscilla to run Rosewood—yet some of them weren't really prepared to let her do that."

Frank shifted in his seat. "Shouldn't the board of directors have input?"

"By all means. But why pay someone thirty-five thousand—hard-to-come-by—dollars a year if you aren't prepared to let them exercise the expertise they were trained for?"

"Do you feel the Board got in the way of Priscilla doing her job?" Frank asked.

"Sometimes, yes."

"Did you ever say as much?"

Irmajean almost felt like Frank was interrogating her. "I tried—but if you ever doubted people hear only what they want to hear, get yourself appointed to a board of directors."

"Who raised the most objections?"

"Barron and Ted. One or the other of them was always claiming things should be thus and so because that's the way they used to be. They've seemed scared to death that I'd make some sweeping changes in the gardens. By the time Chalmers passed away, the property was terribly neglected. So I organized a volunteer staff of local gardeners who were willing to donate their time to bringing the gardens up to snuff. And we were right to do so. People come to see the house, but the big draw is the gardens. More than once someone has paid the fee for a tour of the house, and then said, 'Is that all there is?' But not once has anyone toured the gardens and left anything but satisfied. Plus we rent them out for weddings and teas."

Frank rested his beefy arms on the table after his wife cleared away the dessert plates and refilled everyone's coffee cups. "If the goal was to bring Rosewood up to its original condition why would Ted and Barron or anyone for that matter have any objections?"

Irmajean shook her head. "I don't know. Barron hires a landscaping firm to take care of his own property, and I've heard he complains if a pine needle is left on the lawn. Ted, however, has never done a thing to his property other than having someone mow the grass. He doesn't even like to set foot in Rosewood's garden, and yet, he's always saying to leave things as they were. When we did no more than suggest the possibility of enlarging the Rose Garden, Ted and Barron both objected strenuously."

"How do the others feel?"

"Frederick's main interest is the house. He's done all of the repairs needed, gratis. Plus, he's built a few benches for the garden. He's there working on the house almost as often as I'm there working in the garden."

Glenn interjected a comment. "He does beautiful finish work. The man really has a feel for wood. I know he's bought and rejuvenated a couple of older cottages in town. I appraised one of them, and he had posted a maintenance list for the new owners. Do's and don'ts for maintaining the property. I know for a fact he's taken at least one of the new owners to task because they've put the place in the vacation rental pool. And you know as well as I do that having different people in and out is hard on a house. The new owner was prepared to swear out a complaint against Blumer, but some of the other neighbors talked him out of it. I don't think they were too happy to have the place rented out to somebody different every weekend either."

Frank glanced from Glenn to Irmajean. "You think it's safe to say Frederick becomes overly attached to places? That he might carry that obsession to Rosewood?"

Irmajean didn't want to arouse unnecessary suspicions as far as Frederick or anyone was concerned. "I don't know as how I'd use obsessive to describe how he feels about the property. Passionate perhaps. He's very firm in insisting we respect the age and era of the house. That we can't just willy nilly do things."

Frank leaned away from the table. "Do you think he feels strongly enough that he might have harmed Priscilla when he discovered she'd pulled some of the boards off that attic wall?"

Irmajean shook her head. "If Frederick were guilty of killing Priscilla, he would never have left the wall damaged. He couldn't have stood it."

Frank seemed to be considering the possibility of Frederick Blumer. "Except for that old dog he seems to be a loner."

Jane took exception to her husband's suspicious tone. "Some people prefer their own company, that doesn't make them a criminal. Besides, I've seen him with his dog. That's not a case of master and beast, but true friendship."

Frank patted his wife's hand. "I wasn't suggesting he was guilty of anything. It's just that most of the local contractors and carpenters hang out after hours at the Driftwood Tavern, but I've never seen Frederick darken the door."

"He's a member of Alcoholics Anonymous, which would explain his avoiding the tavern." Glenn surprised everyone with this comment.

They all turned to him, but it was Irmajean who asked, "How did you know that?"

"He told me one time when I was doing an inspection of a house he was working on. I commented on the banister he'd carved, and he said that woodworking and AA had saved him when he was trying to get off the bottle."

Irmajean smiled fondly at her husband. "Sometimes you know the most unlikely things."

Jane picked up the cards and began shuffling them. "That's because Glenn gives the impression secrets are safe with him. And everyone has secrets."

Frank reached over to squeeze his wife's hand. "Except you and me."

Irmajean suspected Frank missed the fleeting expression of sadness that crossed his wife's face after she turned away from him to deal the cards.

Frank seemed to relax his rule about not talking shop during their second rubber of bridge. "Talk to me about Chalmers Carmichael. What did he do to fill his time when he retired?"

Irmajean frowned at a hand that contained only four points. "He talked about writing a local history. He had an extensive collection of books on the area, and he often complained that he thought the important information should be contained in one volume. How far he got with it or even if he started it, I don't know."

Glenn opened with three diamonds, much to Irmajean's wide-eyed chagrin. Not only didn't she have any points to speak of, but she only had a single diamond.

Glenn seemed oblivious to the consternation he'd suddenly caused his wife. "I'm sure Irmajean has mentioned that she worked for Chalmers the last couple of years he operated the paper."

"Did you like working on the paper?" Frank asked.

"Yes, I did. But it wasn't long before I realized *The North Coast Explorer* was a money pit. Costs continued to go up but revenue stayed the same or dropped. Chalmers encouraged advertising, but he kept his rates so low they couldn't begin to fund the rising costs of running a newspaper."

"Why didn't he raise his rates then?"

"Well, Frank, as you know Pirate's Cove is a tourist town, and most of the year there isn't much business. Plus many of the businesses are small. He wanted to encourage them to advertise, and the way to do it was by keeping his rates low. His family originally had quite a lot of money, and I don't think he realized until it was too late that he'd run through a good bit of capital. One of my duties was to keep the books. They were in the red when I took them over and the ink just got redder."

"And he couldn't find a buyer?"

"Not one who stayed interested after they saw the profit and loss statement." With a triumphant slap of the card, she trumped Frank's club ace with a lowly two of diamonds.

He winced and asked, "I've heard people refer to Rosewood as the Carmichael estate. I know that was Chalmers last name and also his mother's before she was married. What's the story there?"

"I'm not sure of the details," Irmajean answered. "Apparently, Clarice's marriage was so unhappy that she resumed her maiden name and Chalmers used it as well."

"Interesting. What can you tell me about Barron Lancaster?"

Irmajean almost wished Frank hadn't asked. She really didn't care for Barron Lancaster, and therefore it was hard to be objective. Maybe a mere recitation of the facts would suffice. "He comes from a pioneer family and seems to think that makes him special. Plus he owns half the town." She glanced over at Mallory. "You know that he's chairman of the Rosewood board of directors?"

"I gathered that when he proceeded to try to run the show this morning. Wouldn't it follow that Priscilla would tell him about any important discovery she might have made?"

Irmajean knew how little Priscilla had liked or respected Barron Lancaster. "I think Priscilla would go for the big coup. A meeting of the entire board."

"Was she a grandstander then?"

Irmajean knew Frank was trying to get a handle on Priscilla's personality. "No, I wouldn't say that, but neither was she a person to hide her light under a bushel."

"So what more can you tell me about Lancaster; old news that I might not know, and that might give me some insight into him as a person."

She tried hard to think of something that would cast a more positive light on Lancaster's character. "Did you happen to notice the tulips? They were magnificent this year. An extravagance really since they have to be replenished frequently if they're going to make a real show. Barron donated the money to buy fifteen hundred tulip bulbs."

Frank all but gulped. "That's a heck of a lot of bulbs."

"Yes, it is. But Barron considers Rosewood a legacy we must maintain. And he remembers that Chalmers' mother planted tulips by the hundreds. Apparently, she held a garden party every spring when the tulips were in all their glory. There was always a striped tent to protect the guests, and the food in case of a rain shower. And, of course, there was always a tour of the gardens. Barron is very fond of remembering how things used to be, and therefore, how they should be now. I don't know if you've ever had the occasion to go inside Barron's home, but it's a time capsule. I always wondered if the reason he never married was because he couldn't find a woman who wanted to double as a museum curator."

"Wait a minute." And Frank held up his hand. "I though Chalmers mother was a very private person, keeping to herself other than at work. And yet you're talking garden parties."

"Well, apparently prior to her marriage, she did quite a bit of entertaining."

"What happened to change things?"

"Her marriage. I don't know any of the details."

"Frank, you can't expect Irmajean to know everything." Jane evidently felt Frank's questioning had gone on long enough.

Glenn laughed. "Not for want of trying."

Irmajean boxed him on the shoulder. "Stop. I can't help it if people tell me things."

"In an effort to get their twisted arms back." But he was grinning when he said it.

Jane laughed and asked, "Do you have any idea why Ted, Chalmers, Barron—none of them ever married? Three eligible bachelors—or so they must have been when they were young."

"Well, I can relate what I've been told. I commented on the fact when we hadn't lived here too long, and remember, we've been here for thirty-four years, so Chalmers would have been in his thirties and Ted and Barron in their forties. I was told in a whispered aside that all three men once loved the same woman. Someone who came for the summer long ago. They were known as the Glamourous Quartet, and they went everywhere together—the Siren from the East and the three bachelors. Supposedly, they courted her as one, and she apparently never singled one out from the others. So maybe it was never anything more than a group flirtation. Fun while it lasted but never intended to go anywhere. And maybe, they've all suffered from a case of unrequited love." She raised her plump shoulders in an eloquent shrug. "I don't suppose after all this time we're apt to find out."

Jane lay her cards down. "So what happened to the Siren from the East?"

Irmajean shrugged. "She went home, I guess. At least she moved out of the picture. And the three bachelors never married. Chalmers ran the family newspaper while Barron managed his family's considerable properties, preserved the family estate, and practiced law. He even served a couple of terms in the state legislature."

"And Ted? What did Ted do?"

"Ted treaded water. He lived off of inherited money while pottering at this and that. Like Barron and Chalmers, he sanctified, and still maintains, the family home although his home was never as grand as Rosewood or Lancaster's. Still, there is considerable property that goes with Ted's house. I've really been surprised that he's

never sold any of it off. At least the timber. Because he
drives an old car, wears his clothes until they're
threadbare, and always orders the cheapest thing on the
menu. I don't think he's ever really held down a paying
job. If he has it's never been long enough for anyone to
notice. But that doesn't make him guilty of anything."

"It seems Ted has made a career out of preserving the
past."

Jane nodded her agreement at Glenn's comment. "For
some tending the past is a full time job in itself."

They played the next hand of cards in silence. But as
the last card was played, Frank returned to the matter of
Rosewood. "It seems likely Priscilla's death had
something to do with Rosewood. Do you know of any
mysteries connected with the house? Anything I might
follow up on?"

Irmajean mentally sorted through what she knew about
Rosewood. "Well, I'm probably reaching, but Chalmers'
mother Clarice had a younger brother who disappeared
when he was barely more than a teenager. According to
what I've been told, he walked away from a good job at
the bank, went off to see the world and never came back.
It was always assumed that he died in some remote corner
of the world."

Jane frowned. "But he wouldn't still be alive."

"No, of course not. But he might have had a family."

"Who've returned to Pirate's Cove and murdered
Priscilla Norris because they want to preserve some
family secret? That doesn't seem very likely." Glenn
shuffled and then dealt the cards.

"At this point I'm willing to consider all possibilities. Can you tell me anything more about this little known brother, Irmajean?"

"Not really. Other than the fact that a great deal was expected of him since he was the son and heir. When he didn't return from wandering, the mantle of family responsibility fell on Clarice's shoulders. She was the older by several years."

"I can add a little bit to that."

They all looked at Glenn in surprise.

"I was doing an appraisal for a long time resident recently who wanted to talk about the history of Pirate's Cove. Actually, he wanted to rehash a lot of old gossip. I only listened with half an ear, but I did pay attention when he started to mention Rosewood. I was going to relate what he said to you, Irmajean, but then I forgot."

"Well, don't forget now, for heaven's sake. What did he say?"

"Well, not much really, except that Clarice's brother left town not so much of his own volition but because he was asked to."

They all looked at him with interest, but it was Frank who said, "Now why was that, I wonder?"

Eleven

Irmajean crawled into bed, settled the pillows comfortably under her head and reached for the paperback mystery that would help her get to sleep. "Do you realize that we never got around to telling Frank about our discovery today? We mentioned we'd found something and then the conversation got sidetracked."

Glenn laid the sci-fi thriller he was reading face down on his chest. "Amusing as they are, Catkin's avenues of transport probably have nothing to with the mystery at Rosewood."

Irmajean realized with regret that he was probably right. When she finally fell asleep, it was to dream of Catkin. However a Catkin far different from the one she knew. In her dream, he could talk and kept saying he had something to show her. When she awoke, it was to find Chunky Monkey, her own big orange Tom, sleeping on her chest. Perhaps he was to blame for her peculiar dream.

~ * ~

Morning dawned fine and sunny. Glenn was up first and the smell of coffee drifted through the house.

Irmajean came downstairs with two yowling cats in attendance.

"Haven't you fed these beasties, yet?"

"Yes, they just want you to think I haven't."

Irmajean gently shooed Emily from the cushion of her chair and sat down. "I'm going back out to Rosewood and finish searching the office. Do you want to come with me?"

"Can't." There was genuine regret in his voice. "I've got an appraisal I have to get out today. But you be careful. Keep the doors locked and if anything doesn't look right, you call the police."

"I will, but don't worry. I'm sure there will be people coming and going. Those that have a right to be there and then the morbidly curious."

However, when Irmajean unlocked the door to Rosewood's office she was immediately struck by the silence of the house. She tried to rationalize that the quiet was a good thing because it surely meant she was as alone. But it also made it difficult to concentrate because she found herself stopping every so often to simply listen. Finally, she decided to go upstairs and make herself a cup of tea. The sounds of water running and then heating in the kettle brought a semblance of life to the disturbingly quiet old house.

While she waited for the teakettle to whistle, Irmajean checked Catkin's food supply. She'd filled his bowl yesterday, and it was now empty so he was managing access to it some way. But then access to anywhere he wanted seemed to be Catkin's modus operandi.

She was in the process of absently dipping her tea bag up and down when there was a pounding on the door of the office. A glance out the window, which overlooked the parking area, showed that a maroon van identical to the one Jim Mills drove was parked beside her own car. It was the middle of the week and school wasn't out yet. So what was he doing there? Playing hooky? And after raising such a fuss about taking time off to attend the board meeting.

Leaving her tea to cool, Irmajean descended the stairs to the office and saw that, sure enough, Jim Mills was on the other side of the locked door. Just as she was about to open it, he leaned close to the glass and peered in. He didn't look any too happy, but then she reminded herself he never did.

Once she'd unlocked the door, he began a verbal barrage that reminded her how much she disliked him. "I thought that was your car. What took you so long to answer the door?" He didn't bother to say hello, as he pushed past her and into the office.

"I was upstairs." It was all the explanation he was going to get.

He walked past her and over to the Director's desk, turned the file around she'd been looking through and shuffled the pages while he took a quick look. Making her long to slap his hands. "What makes you so special, Irmajean, that you have access to this place while the rest of us are locked out?"

"I wouldn't say you were locked out, Jim."

"I'd certainly like to know what you call it then."

"Is there something I can do to help you?" Irmajean found herself wishing she'd ignored the knocking at the door and paid attention to her tea which was growing cold while she was a captive audience for Jim Mills' rudeness.

"Priscilla promised to lend me some books. I've come for them."

He was too self-absorbed to realize that her hackles rose at his presumptuousness. "Do you need them right this minute? I don't think Chief Mallory would want anything leaving the house right now."

"It's just a couple of history books for God's sake! I built my last two weeks of lesson plans around them."

Irmajean watched as he moved restlessly around the room, lifting anything that was exposed and having a look at it. He gave the definite impression of a man searching for something, but she would doubt very much that it was history books. "How could you have built lessons around something you don't have, Jim?"

"They're pioneer diaries, and I was going to read to the kids out of them. It's pretty hard to hold their interest this late in the year, and I thought they might get a kick out of the trials and tribulations of some of our early settlers. Not to mention the down right laughable use of grammar and spelling."

She couldn't believe this man had the audacity to call himself a history teacher. How in the world had he ever gotten on the board for Rosewood with an attitude like that? She knew many of Chalmer's books were valuable and doubted Jim Mills would show them the proper respect. At any rate, she certainly wasn't going to give him permission to take anything—not even the garbage, away from Rosewood. "Wouldn't these diaries be available through the local library?"

"Not these particular ones, no. The ones I'm after are original copies. Probably one-of-a-kind."

Alarm bells went off in Irmajean's head. "If they're one-of-a-kind, I doubt that you should be taking them off the premises. Surely Priscilla wouldn't have allowed it. She was more protective of Rosewood than a mother hen of her chicks."

Mills didn't meet her gaze with his own. "But Priscilla isn't around to raise any objections, is she?"

Irmajean drew herself up into what Honey liked to call her prim librarian pose. Only minutes ago Mills was claiming that Priscilla had given him permission to borrow the books. "No, she isn't *around,* as you put it, Jim. But I think we should pay her memory some respect by honoring the things she tried to do for this property. I'm not going to allow you to take anything away. Even if Priscilla gave you written permission. Since Chief Mallory isn't present to remind you, I will, that this is a crime scene."

"Yeah, well, she wasn't murdered in the library. So how about letting me have a look around for what I want, and maybe I can photocopy enough to get me by. Surely you can't object to that?"

Irmajean thought she might very well object, when the dratted phone began ringing. She considered ignoring it, and then realized it might be Glenn calling. He'd be out in a flash, taking the corners at breakneck speed, endangering life and limb, if she didn't answer. "Wait right here, Jim, while I answer the phone." But of course he paid absolutely no attention to what she said, making a dash for the stairs as soon as she picked up the telephone. And since it was Chief Mallory and not her husband, she couldn't very well hang up on him with the admonition she'd call right back, although she could darn well alert him to what was happening.

"Frank, I'm glad you called."

He didn't miss the urgency in her voice. "What's up?"

"Jim Mills is here, and he insists Priscilla was going to loan him some books from Chalmers' collection. Frank, I don't feel right about this. I know Chalmers had some extremely valuable volumes on local history. You know, one-of-a-kind or limited edition. Titles rare book collectors might kill for." As soon as the words were out of her mouth, she realized their implication.

"Are you suggesting..."

"No, I'm not suggesting that's what happened. But I am saying I don't think Jim should be allowed to take anything from the premises. No matter what Priscilla might have promised him. I've told him as much, but I'm not so sure he intends listening to me."

"Then tell him *I* said he wasn't to touch a thing. That technically he's trespassing on a crime scene. That personally he's casting some very serious suspicions on himself. With any luck, one of those three should warn him off, but I suggest the board get somebody in to value those books. Maybe you should give Barron Lancaster a call. After you get rid of Mills." Realizing the position he was putting her in, he added, "I can be out there in ten minutes if you'd like."

Was she really afraid of Jim Mills? "No, I think I can deal with him."

"Good girl. I'll be by sometime this morning."

Irmajean could hear the creak of boards overhead, the tell-tale giveaway in old houses that someone was moving about. Any hope she'd had that Mills might have fled the scene, vanished. Muttering to herself, she made certain the office door was locked and then climbed the stairs to the main floor.

By the time she reached the library, she was breathless with indignation. Jim was there, all right, perched atop the ladder that gave access to the upper most shelves. He clutched several volumes in his arms, while one fragile volume lay askew on the floor, pages loose and binding split. Carefully she picked it up, righted the pages, smoothed the cover and laid the book on a nearby table, all the while counting to ten several times. Irmajean, her voice trembling with anger. ordered. "Jim Mills, put those books back and get down from there this instant."

"Look, I'll bring 'em back."

"I don't care what your intentions are, you're leaving the premises empty handed. And if my authority isn't enough, that was Chief Mallory on the phone, and he says to remind you you're interfering with a crime scene."

Sweat beaded the man's brow, and she could see his hands shaking. There was an urgency about him that outweighed a teacher's need for resource material. Irmajean wondered if Jim Mills had troubles of some kind and was attempting to harvest Rosewood's library in an attempt to solve them? Suddenly Irmajean wasn't so sure this was an incident she wanted to handle by herself.

Much to her relief, Mills laid the books he was holding on the top step of the library ladder. Then he descended the steps. "You're making something out of nothing and, so help me, if I have a visit from the police over this I'm going to hold you responsible."

"If you have a visit from the police, Jim, the only person responsible will be you. If you'd left when I asked you to, we wouldn't be having this confrontation. Now, let's be on your way." She made shooing motions with her hands and assumed a confidence she wasn't feeling.

He gave her a poisonous look and stomped toward the front door, with her hurrying to catch up. "Are you going to walk with me to my car? Hold the door open for me to get in?" He taunted sarcastically.

Irmajean decided to call his bluff. "I think maybe I will. Just to make sure you don't lose your way." She didn't want him circling around and creeping back into the house.

As she would have expected, Jim's car, like him, was untidy. Empty coffee cups, take-out food containers, and crumpled cigarette packages littered the floor. On the dash, reposed several of the plastic cards serious gamblers used in casino slot machines. She recognized two of them as belonging to the casinos within easy driving distance from Pirate's Cove. If Jim Mills had a problem, she would be willing to bet it was gambling.

As soon as the dust from his vehicle settled, Irmajean reentered the house, locking the door behind her. Then she picked up on Chief Mallory's advice and checking the list of board members and their telephone numbers posted by Priscilla's desk, picked up the phone and punched in Barron Lancaster's office number. Naturally his secretary answered.

"I'd like to speak to Barron please."

"Who may I say is calling?"

"Irmajean Lloyd and tell him I'm calling from Rosewood on a matter of some importance." If possible, she didn't want to have to wait for a call back.

"One moment, please." And the secretary put her on hold, but thankfully without any elevator music.

After only a few moments, Lancaster came on the line. "Irmajean, what can I do for you?"

"There's been an incident here at Rosewood, and as a result Frank Mallory suggested I give you a call."

"What's happened?"

Should she try to spare Jim Mills any further trouble by not mentioning his name or should she figure it served him right? "Someone came by and insisted that Priscilla had given them permission to borrow some local history volumes from the library."

"You didn't let this person take anything did you?" His tone was sharp and accusing.

"No, I managed—with a verbal warning from the Chief—to convince them it was in their best interest to leave empty handed. The point of this call is to see if you want to authorize someone to appraise the collection. Also to put you on notice that it has attracted attention."

"If we're going to keep Rosewood alive, we need to protect all of its assets. You were right to give me a call. I know the value of the library is considerable. Why don't I call Ted and have him start to work on cataloguing the books? It's exactly the kind of detail work he excels at, and I would say he's the logical choice giving his familiarity with the property."

Irmajean thought how cleverly this would put Ted back on the scene. Except Frank hadn't wanted anyone but her on the property for several days. "We should okay this with Frank Mallory first?"

"Irmajean, really, what could you have to fear from Ted?"

"I wasn't suggesting I had anything to fear, but since he's temporarily barred from the office I wondered if that might not extend to the rest of the house as well." She could envision him drawing himself up to protest.

"Irmajean, you told me only minutes ago that Mallory suggested you call me. So how could he object to Ted? At least he knows what to expect from Ted."

He had her there.

"Fine. Since you can think of no further objections, why don't you call Ted and ask him to get started."

A sudden thud coming from overhead stopped any further argument on Irmajean's part. Without comment, she hung up the phone and swallowed against an unwelcome bubble of fear, until she reminded herself that she'd undoubtedly heard one of two things. Jim Mills had left in a hurry, but not before he'd wreaked havoc amongst the top shelves. He hadn't bothered or offered to replace the books he'd pulled from their places once she'd ordered him out of the house. No doubt some of the teetering volumes had tumbled to the floor. Either that or Catkin was up to some mischief. At least Catkin had furry cuteness going for him, which as she huffed up the stairs to the main floor was definitely more than could be said for weasely Jim Mills.

Irmajean had just reached the library when she heard a loud knocking at the basement door. She glared back in the direction she'd just come and would have let whoever knock until their knuckles ached when a glance out the window—identified her caller as the police. Resigned, she retraced her steps to let Chief Mallory inside.

"I was beginning to wonder where you were."

"Upstairs, checking on the damage Jim Mills set in motion." There was another thud from overhead. "See what I mean? He removed some of the books from a top shelf and now other volumes have been toppling off. I was on my way to set things right when you arrived."

"I thought you sounded worried on the telephone so I decided to drive out."

Irmajean saw no need in denying the obvious. "The situation did make me a bit uneasy. Priscilla may very well have told Jim he could borrow some books, although I doubt it. If we let them walk out the door we might not see them again." Should she voice her concerns about Jim? "Furthermore, when I followed Jim out to his car I wondered if he might be planning on borrowing the books permanently. He was exhibiting too much anxiety for a teacher wanting research material. Have you ever heard that he has a gambling problem?" She went on to describe what she'd seen in Jim's vehicle.

"I've heard rumors he likes to gamble. Sounds like he might be into something he can't control. I think you shouldn't waste any time getting someone in here to evaluate the library. That way we'll know if something turns up missing."

"I called Barron as you suggested. He in turn recommended Ted as the logical choice to catalogue the books. But I wanted to clear it with you, although Barron argued that it wasn't necessary." It annoyed her that she was rarely a verbal match for the arrogant attorney.

"I think it's all right to let Ted take on the library. I don't think we have anything to fear from him, and that way, you wouldn't be alone in the house while you continue going over the office. I take it you haven't found anything or you would have said."

"Actually, yes." She stood aside in the hall and waited for him to come along side. "We intended mentioning it last night, but you know how our conversations sometimes go off in different directions."

He nodded.

"I don't know if any of this will be helpful, but we did find some newspaper clippings where Priscilla had highlighted reference to a garden maze at Rosewood. So now we know the basis for the notation in her diary. And since she hadn't told me before I left on vacation, I would assume the discovery was recent."

"Okay. Anything else?"

"Well, we managed to solve the mystery as to how Catkin gets to point A from point C when he's denied access to point B."

"I didn't realize this was an issue."

"His comings and goings have often puzzled me. He's using the heating ducts for the original heating system. The one in the office is minus its cover."

"Leave it to a cat. Are these big enough for a person to crawl through by any chance?"

Irmajean shook her head. "A small child, maybe, but not an adult. I know it probably means nothing to the investigation." Her voice dwindled off.

Another thud greeted them as they entered the library, a medium-sized room with the walls almost covered in ceiling to floor bookshelves. A bay window allowed sunlight into the room, which smelled pleasantly of old books. The library ladder was still in place, but several volumes were now scattered on the floor and a totally unrepentant cat perched on the top shelf. The books that now littered the floor had blocked a heating duct.

Irmajean bent down to pick up the books. "You're a bad cat. Honestly, he does get into mischief. But I've never known him to do this before, maybe that's because the books blocked it tightly until Jim got his hands on them."

Frank relieved her of her load. "Here, let me put those back on the shelf."

"Gladly, my equilibrium isn't the best when I get very far off the ground."

Irmajean watched as Catkin disappeared once more within the walls of Rosewood. Frank packed the books tightly together as she handed them up to him. The last one was a small, fat photo album.

"Is that it for the books?"

"There's one more, a photograph album, but I think I'll take a look at it first. Can you keep Catkin's route blocked without it?"

"I'll just take a book from the next shelf down." He descended the ladder then wiped his hands on his pants. "It's been a heckava long time since anybody's dusted up there." He glanced around at the hundreds of old books lining the walls of the library. "This family didn't go in much for light reading, did they?"

"Novels are on shelves in the bedrooms. I know Chalmers was proud of his collection. I can remember him saying more than once that books were his only vice."

"Don't you ever wonder about people like Chalmers, Barron and Ted? Men, and women, too, who lead quiet lives, living on old money, surrounding themselves with books and the residue of the past? Did they—do they ever want the things you and I take for granted, like a life's companion?"

Irmajean knew exactly what Frank meant. "I wouldn't think being a musty old bachelor held much appeal, but during the time I worked with Chalmers I came to realize that his life was anything but empty." Irmajean hugged the photo album to her bosom while she looked back into the past and her many conversations with Chalmers Carmichael. "He and Millicent were quite good friends, you know. Once a week they shared dinner and then read to each other."

This piece of information clearly surprised Frank. "She must have had fifteen, twenty years on him. What kind of literature could they possibly have had in common? Look at the books lining his walls and she writes those—those raunchy romances." Then he quickly added, "Or so I've been told."

"Mysteries. That's what they had in common. They were both crazy about them. In Chalmers case, the enthusiasm is in the past tense. Although maybe not. Who can say for sure what we'll be reading in the next world?"

Frank frowned. "Yeah, well, I'll worry about that when the time comes. Well, I guess I'd best get going. Give Ted a call and have him get busy on the library."

"I'll call him right now."

Irmajean locked the office door behind the police chief and then dialed Ted's phone number.

It was taking Ted forever to answer the telephone, and she was about to hang up when he finally picked up, obviously out of breath. "Hello."

"Ted, this is Irmajean. I'm glad I caught you."

"I was just coming in the door. Grocery shopping day you know. It's the day the local market gives a ten percent discount to senior citizens."

Irmajean nodded even though Ted couldn't see her. She knew he pinched every penny until it hollered. "Ted, Chief Mallory just left, and he suggested I call you and ask you for some help."

"I wondered when he would realize how important I am to Rosewood. I can come over as soon as I put my groceries away."

She could tell by the sound of his voice that her comment had him preening. "That would be wonderful, but first let me tell you briefly what I want."

"I assumed you wanted some help in the office." His tone was a tad tart.

"That's always valuable of course, but specifically we were wondering if you could catalogue the library. I can explain in detail when you get here, but we're afraid somebody might be trying to steal some of the books."

He positively screeched. "You mustn't let anyone in that room!" The alarm in his voice was genuine. "You're not speaking in the past tense when you say that someone might try to steal some of the books? You were speaking hypothetically weren't you?" His tone begged for reassurance.

Irmajean knew Ted was genuinely alarmed at the thought of anyone taking books from the library. "Not exactly, no." She didn't think Jim Mills had managed to get away with anything, but then she couldn't be certain that he hadn't secreted some slim volume in a pocket or inside his shirt. He'd clearly been desperate enough to try anything short of bashing her over the head, and she wasn't even too sure about that. She'd been careful not to turn her back on him.

"Not exactly! Irmajean, do you really think someone took books from the library?"

"Ted, why don't you put your groceries away and come down to Rosewood. Then I can tell you what happened, and you can tell me if you think any damage has been done. You sound as if you might have an idea what books were there."

"Please don't use the past tense in the same breath with Chalmers' library. He had a definitive collection and yes, I know what was there. Down to the last volume, because he had me catalogue it the year he sold the paper. And believe me it was of considerable value. Some volumes were priceless in that they were irreplaceable. One-of-a-kind old diaries, self-published local histories. I recommended to Chalmers that some of them should be under lock and key, but he wouldn't hear of it. He said I was the only person besides him who knew what he had, and he trusted me as much as he trusted himself." His voice trembled with anxiety. "Irmajean, has something happened?"

"Listen, Ted, relax. We'll go over everything when you get here. I'm assuming since you catalogued it that there's a list of the collection somewhere."

"There is—I'll bring it with me."

He hung up the phone before Irmajean could say anything more, but as she replaced the telephone receiver, she wondered why Barron hadn't mentioned that Ted had already inventoried the library?

While she waited for Ted, she searched through some more of the filing cabinets. She was beginning to tire of the search and long for a search of another kind—that of a

garden maze. When Ted came bursting into the office, she
jumped a foot.

His panic was obvious, if a bit melodramatic. She
couldn't imagine anything in Chalmers' library worth
quite this much alarm. But then Ted knew what was there
and she didn't.

He clutched a vinyl bound pamphlet. "I have a listing
of the entire contents of the library right here. Now tell me
what has happened."

"Really, Ted, I don't think there's any reason to be
quite so alarmed." She felt the absurd need to pat his hand
and reassure him everything was all right.

"Let me be the judge of that, Irmajean Lloyd. You may
know a lot more about flowers than I do, but I know a
thing or two about old books."

He hurried past her to climb the stairs to the main floor.
Irmajean slammed shut the file drawer that had occupied
her and hurried after him. Only seconds had elapsed, but
he was already pushing the ladder into place and
mounting the steps.

"Someone has been in here. I can tell at a glance that
the books are out of place." He glared at her. "It wasn't
you was it?"

"No, no—Ted be careful on that thing?" Her warning
came after he missed a step in his haste and almost fell.

Ted ran his finger along the spines of the top shelf
books. The ones Catkin had knocked off and Jim Mills
had tried to borrow. If Ted knew as much as he wanted
her to think he'd know that the photograph album was
missing. But was anything else?

"These books have been disarranged. Did you do it?"

Irmajean felt no loyalty to Jim Mills turned Dr. Hyde and saw no reason to beat around the bush in explaining to Ted what had happened. "Jim Mills came by and insisted Priscilla had given him permission to borrow some of the books from the library for use in a classroom lecture. I told him I couldn't sanction such a loan, but before I could show him the door, Chief Mallory called. Jim took advantage of this distraction to make a beeline for the library."

"You didn't let him take anything did you?" Ted's voice was positively accusing.

"I did my level best to prevent him, and I think I succeeded unless he managed to secret something on his person. But he certainly was angry."

Ted descended the ladder. "I can't tell if anything is missing until I consult my list, but the books are loose enough on the shelf that I'm sure something has been taken."

Irmajean knew she might as well confess now as later. "I borrowed a photograph album. It tumbled to the floor…" She noticed Ted wince and close his eyes as if he was in pain. She refrained from adding that it had been Catkin who knocked it off, not Jim. After all, Jim Mills had started the trouble. Catkin had only seized a well-presented opportunity. "You know you can trust me, Ted. I wanted to see if there were some early pictures of the garden."

"I'm not worried about you, Irmajean. But Jim Mills is a different story. I'll never know how he wormed his way onto the board. We need to be a lot more careful who we appoint to serve on the board of Rosewood. There are enough qualified people in this community that we don't need to open our doors to every piece of flotsam and jetsam that ends up on our doorstep." He took a large handkerchief from his pocket and wiped his brow, then polished his glasses. "This collection is irreplaceable, literally. If it's made available to anyone it should only be true scholars and, even then, only under close supervision."

"Ted, how valuable is the library?"

"There are some single volumes worth thousands of dollars each."

Irmajean gasped. "And we've just left them sitting on the shelves?" She thought of the countless tour groups that had passed through the house. People with backpacks and oversized purses. The thought made her positively lightheaded.

"I tried to persuade Chalmers to take reasonable precautions when he was alive. I failed. Priscilla knew the library was valuable, and her credentials convinced Barron to have the insurance increased to cover them. A necessary precaution, but one that ate into our already slender resources." He sank down onto an uncomfortable looking chair with a faded needlepoint cushion. "Barron had discussed finances with Priscilla, but I don't think they had reached the point of sharing with anyone else. Although I knew of course, that the coffers were getting low. Some of the investments hadn't paid off as hoped. I really don't see how we can afford to replace Priscilla.

Not if we're going to keep Rosewood open. Priscilla and I didn't always see eye to eye on things, but I know she had agreed to a cut in salary. She was passionate in her devotion to Rosewood—and so well-qualified." The latter was a rare and posthumous compliment on Ted's part.

All of this was news to Irmajean and conjured up a hard lump in her chest. Had Priscilla's killer not only robbed that young woman of a future, but Rosewood as well? She ventured the only obvious alternative. "Perhaps we can find someone less expensive." But that might mean far less qualified.

"Or a volunteer or volunteers to oversee things."

"Ted, I don't think that would work. Somebody qualified needs to be in charge on a full time basis. Volunteers need coordinating."

"You could do it, Irmajean. You're here much of the time anyway."

There was a note of desperation in his voice, and she wondered if Rosewood meant that much to him or if it was something else. He'd certainly never given her the impression he thought her competent to run anything. "Ted, I have no desire to be the Director of Rosewood, paid or otherwise. While I think the house is a wonderful old place that should be preserved, my interest is in the gardens. If I were trying to run this place, I'd never have any time for them. Besides," and she almost lost the battle not to reach over and pat his hand reassuringly. "We're not out in the streets yet. We can charge a little more for the tours, and we haven't even begun to have much in the way of fundraisers. The garden is looking better all the time, and soon the rose garden will be ready for teas. That kind of thing has become quite popular again, as are gardens." Then as a little jog to his memory she added, "Just think, Ted, if we could locate and recreate the original garden maze what a draw that would be. I found proof in some old newspapers that there really was one here on Rosewood's property. Now we just have to find it."

She had meant to be reassuring, but the eyes he turned toward her were troubled. "We'll save Rosewood, Ted. Don't worry."

To her great surprise, he grabbed her hand and clutched it as if she might unexpectedly flee the room. "We have to, Irmajean. It would be a disaster if we were forced to sell and strangers moved onto the property."

"Yes, well—" And this time she gave into temptation and did pat his hand. "We won't let that happen." She managed to disentangle herself from Ted's grasp. "Now, I have a little more work to do in the office, so I'll leave you to the library."

"It could take days to check the entire inventory." His voice was almost a wail.

"For the whole library, yes. But Jim Mills got no further than those top two shelves."

~ * ~

Irmajean had just finished a fruitless search of the last filing cabinet when Ted joined her. "Well?"

"There are two volumes missing from that section, besides the photograph album you have. There's a one-of-a-kind dictionary of Chinook jargon compiled by

Chalmers' grandmother. Local Indians as well as early
settlers and traders used the dialect. So little knowledge of
it remains. And it would fetch a nice price in the rare book
trade."

Irmajean knew she'd done all she could in trying to
prevent Jim Mills from taking anything. None the less, she
felt guilty. If any of the library contents were to be sold, it
should be to benefit Rosewood, not support someone's
gambling habit. "What else is missing?"

"A book entitled *Architecture, Mysticism and Myth.*
It's of no consequence as regards local history, but it was
printed in the late 1800's. It seems an odd choice for Mills
to take when there were so many obviously valuable
books at his fingertips."

A disquieting thought crossed Irmajean's mind. Could
someone else have taken that book? She picked up the
telephone and dialed the number of the police station.
"We—you need to report this, Ted. Perhaps they can
intercept Jim before he has a chance to dispose of them."
When Frank Mallory came on the line, she handed the
phone to Ted. Once that was done, he took his leave and
she locked up after him. Then climbed the stairs to the
main floor and made certain there was food for the cat and
that all the doors were bolted.

As she passed the library, she wondered if Ted had
thought to look under any of the furniture for the missing
books. She recalled how some had been scattered on the
floor when she finally managed to evict Jim Mills. "I'll
just have a look," she thought aloud.

With some effort, she got down on her hands and knees, lifted the skirt of the sofa and peered under it. Nothing but dust. However, from this vantage point she could see behind one of the curtains. There was something there. Struggling to her feet, she went over to move the heavy drapery and revealed a small book. She hoped it was the Chinook jargon dictionary but was disappointed. *Architecture, Mysticism and Myth* wasn't a very big book, almost pocket size in fact, but it was well read and contained several bookmarks.

Curious, she carried it over to a comfortable chair and sat down. The book fell open easily to a chapter entitled *The Labyrinth*. This had obviously been of interest to someone because it was underlined and crabbed notes written in the margins. She hadn't been Chalmers Carmichael's Girl Friday for several years without becoming totally familiar with his constipated handwriting. Labyrinths, mazes, the unknown—where, she wondered, did they all fit in to the history of Rosewood?

Twelve

Irmajean sat up in bed, a plethora of pillows supporting her and Emily the calico batting at her toes as she wiggled them under the covers. "I'm missing something—"

"What? What are you missing?" Glenn glanced up from the science fiction book he was reading. "I wasn't aware you'd lost anything."

"That's not the kind of missing I mean. I'm referring to Rosewood. There's a lot of odd behavior going on that I can't put into perspective. Ted is jumpy as the dickens, and whenever he and Barron are together they keep exchanging meaningful looks. Then there's Frederick claiming there are underground tunnels. I've never heard a single hint of such a thing. Then, of course, there's Jim who was all but frothing at the mouth when he was at Rosewood today. And Rose is still unaccounted for."

Glenn marked his place with his thumb. "What do you think you might be missing?"

"I haven't a clue. I've turned Priscilla's office upside down, and I'm still no closer to knowing why she was murdered."

Realizing this conversation wasn't going to be over any time soon, Glenn placed a bookmark in his book and laid it on the nightstand. "Maybe the answer doesn't lie in the office. The only clue Priscilla left was her notation to tell you about the maze."

Irmajean scooted against the pillows so she'd be facing him. "I know—and I thought I might find something related to that in the office. But no luck."

"You could try looking in the garden."

"Honey, I've been through the garden a zillion times and seen absolutely nothing even remotely resembling a maze. I'm stymied as to what to do next."

"Leave the investigation to Frank."

She gave her husband a disgruntled look. "Frank didn't know Priscilla and has no idea how to deal with our board of directors. He asked me for help and he's going to get it."

"Irmajean, he asked you to look over the office—not oversee the investigation."

"You and I are just doing a little brainstorming. There's no harm in that."

"As long as that's all it is."

"I wish I understood why Ted is in such a panic over the future of the estate. Today he tried to persuade me to be volunteer director, because he's convinced there aren't enough funds to hire another professional. I tried to put his mind at ease by telling him we hadn't begun to tap the fund raising potential Priscilla had mapped out for us. He doesn't want to see the house pass into the hands of strangers—he almost has apoplexy at the thought—and yet, he isn't willing to implement everything that might keep the property in the hands of the historical society. He continues to deny knowing anything about a garden maze."

"Don't you think Ted is just being Ted?"

"I suppose there's always that possibility. And maybe I'm adding two and two and coming up with five."

"There's always that possibility."

"You're no help."

Honey reached optimistically for his book. "Every great detective needs a devil's advocate."

"You think you're up to playing Hastings or Watson, do you?"

"Anything you want, dear. Anything you want."

"No."

He laid his book back down. "No? No, what?"

"No, I don't think Ted is just being Ted. Something has him scared, and I think it's something he doesn't want anyone to find out." She let him be then, while she turned the pages of the photograph album she'd brought home from Rosewood.

She'd thought there might be a picture of the garden maze, but while there were lots of snapshots taken in the garden, they seemed to showcase women with big hats and men with serious expressions and bushy mustaches. The women's fashions were a good gauge of the decade when they were taken. Hemlines moved upward and millinery confections disappeared, while the men in the photos seemed less severe and the women positively coquettish. Some of the faces began to look familiar. "Honey, look at this. Who does it look like?"

Glenn turned over to rest on his elbow and study the face indicated by the tip of Irmajean's finger. "It looks like Millicent Morgan, but is that possible?"

"I think so. She brags about being eighty-two, but this picture could easily have been taken when she was a teenager"

The old photographs *were* interesting, and he began turning the pages back toward the beginning, pausing every so often to study an image. "You know what I find interesting? The same face appears in the background of several of the snapshots." He tapped one in particular. "Did you know that Chalmers' family had an Asian servant?"

"No, I didn't." She turned the album so she could have a better look. "You're right. The same man is visible in the background of several of the pictures. He seems to always be carrying a tray. Now why do you suppose no one has ever mentioned him?"

"Why not ask Ted?"

"I will. But it will probably be an exercise in futility. He seems to have erased the past from his memory banks." Irmajean reached over and turned off the light.

~ * ~

She awoke to another fine morning. Birds were calling to one another, the ocean was a gentle song in the background and the sky was an incredible shade of blue. She showered and dressed, filling the over-sized pockets of her garden smock with the usual odds and ends, including a pair of shears and some twine. Then she hurried downstairs to breakfast. She was just biting into a cranberry scone when a knock came at the door.

Glenn lowered the newspaper and glanced her way. "Now who can that be this early?"

Irmajean abandoned her scone and went to answer the door. Frank Mallory stood on the porch. "I won't stay long, but I wondered if you'd found anything else of interest at Rosewood."

"I don't know how pertinent it is to the investigation, but I did find something interesting in that photograph album Catkin dislodged. I'll show you. Actually, Glenn is the one who noticed it. Sit down, have a cup of coffee, and I'll be right back."

She pushed back her chair and went upstairs to retrieve the album from beside the bed where it was laying in a puddle of sunlight with a cat curled on top. Gently dislodging Smokey, the shy gray stray they'd adopted, she picked up the album and headed back downstairs.

She returned with the photo album, placed it in front of Frank and turned to the pages in question. "There's an Asian servant in several of the photographs. We assumed he was a servant because he's always holding a tray and is always in the background apart from the smiling crowd. As if his being in the pictures was incidental. I think it's curious no mention is made of him—anywhere."

"Maybe it's because the people who could afford servants liked to pretend they were invisible."

"Maybe so..." But she wasn't convinced.

"So, am I to assume you've finished going over the office?"

"Yes, I am."

"Wanna have a look for the garden maze?"

Irmajean couldn't believe her luck.

After Frank departed and before she left for Rosewood, Irmajean placed a call to Millicent Morgan. Perhaps she would recall that long ago garden party and the unknown man standing in the shadows behind her. As she listened to the phone ring, Irmajean thought about all the people now connected with Rosewood who had been connected with the property in the past. Everyone of them had been silent about some aspects of this connection. Why? Was there a link between this silence and Priscilla's murder?

"Good morning."

"Millicent, hello. This is Irmajean Lloyd." Irmajean knew that Millicent's real name was Gertrude, but that the romance writer had adopted Millicent as more befitting a successful author. And Millicent *was* successful. Her novels had provided her with a lavish retirement that her years as a schoolteacher could never have made possible. Once her books had begun to sell, Gertrude had legally changed her name to Millicent.

"Irmajean! What can I do for you?"

Millicent's voice was enthusiastic and Irmajean suspected she didn't receive many telephone calls. At eighty-two, Millicent had outlived most of her contemporaries. Besides that, her chosen profession required she spend a certain amount of time on her own, creating. She attended church every Sunday and all events at Rosewood. Usually among the first to arrive and always one of the last to leave. Without fail, she wore a hat on her snowy white curls and gloves on her small white hands. She was a relic from another time, and Irmajean hoped to unlock some of the memories she had to have stored away.

"Millicent, I was wondering if you'd be free to have lunch with me today or tomorrow. I'm really upset over the goings on at Rosewood and thought perhaps we could discuss what's been happening."

"Oh, my dear Irmajean. I'd love to have lunch with you. I don't know what Rosewood will do without Priscilla."

"We'll have trouble replacing her that's for certain, but I know when the time comes that your input will be valuable."

"Why, Irmajean, thank you." Millicent's voice sounded as if she was positively preening. "Might I suggest we meet at the Cottage Tea Room?"

The elegant little establishment was exactly where you might expect to find Millicent, her hat in place and her white gloves laid delicately beside her plate. "Perfect. Shall we say at one?"

"I'll look forward to it."

Irmajean hung up the phone, satisfied that she was making progress, although she wasn't exactly sure in what direction.

Irmajean busied herself around the house until time to meet Millicent. In keeping with the spirit of the event, she decided to wear her garden hat, sprucing it up with a burgundy velvet rose that matched her dress. She turned round and round before the mirror and decided she didn't look half bad. Glenn wandered in and smiled his approval. "You look nice."

"Thank you. I'm having lunch with Millicent at the Cottage Tea Room, and you know what an elegant little place that is. Besides Millicent always wears a hat and gloves. Unfortunately the only gloves I possess are designed solely for the garden." She glanced around. "Does this rose Gemma sent me look all right?" Gemma was the eldest by twenty minutes of their twin daughters and had made it her mission to glamorize her mother.

"You look fine."

"Then I'd best be off."

"Why this sudden friendship with Millicent Morgan?"

"Here's a woman who's lived in this town for eighty-two years, and nobody thinks to ask her what she remembers. We both recognized her in that picture taken at Rosewood, so I'm hoping she might be able to fill in some of the blanks concerning the estate."

"I guess that sounds harmless enough. Well, have a good time."

The Cottage Tea Room was tucked away on a side street and almost lost beneath a smothering bower of roses. Irmajean saw Millicent had procured a prime table by one of the room's two bay windows. From there they could look out on a tiny but nearly perfect garden of seemingly endless blooms. The proprietor of Rose Cottage was a great chef with a green thumb. Millicent smiled as Irmajean sat down across from her. "Oh, Irmajean, I love what you've done with your hat! That rose is much better than that slightly bedraggled bird."

That slightly bedraggled bird was an old friend. "Thank you—I think."

"Oh, dear! I didn't mean that to be insulting. I really meant that you looked quite perfect for tea at the Cottage."

"Thank you, Millicent, and so do you." She glanced around the room. It really was a charming spot. Set on plumbing the depths of Millicent's memory Irmajean began by asking, "I imagine this must remind you of the tea parties once held at Rosewood."

Millicent flushed. "Oh, well I..."

Irmajean continued on as if she hadn't the faintest suspicion Millicent might be about to deny what she knew to be the truth. "Catkin dislodged a row of books in the library the other day, a photograph album among them. I'm afraid I couldn't resist looking through the album at pictures of the good old days. You can imagine how pleased I was to recognize you in one of the photographs. Social engagements at that elegant house would have suited you."

"Well, I—I wasn't invited to many of them. I was friends with Chalmers' mother, although she was a good deal older than I. Such a gracious lady." Millicent's faded blue eyes took on a dreamy look. "She would host an annual benefit for the library and garden parties in the summer, and then she would have the monthly meetings of the local literary society. Of which I was a member. We had the best times discussing literature." Her eyes sparkled at remembrance of a happy time. "Listening to and remembering what people liked and didn't like in stories has proved invaluable to me in my own writing."

Irmajean suspected she was right. A good listener could learn a lot. "I'm sure it did."

Millicent nodded and her navy blue straw hat bobbed on her snowy curls. "We had some wonderful times, reading the classics, dressing up, sipping tea from bone china cups. It seems to me now to have been a pleasanter, more gracious era." A look of sadness marred her previously happy expression. "Things changed however when Clarice—Chalmers mother," she added by way of clarification, "married."

"Oh?" Irmajean had to wait for an answer while their waitress placed an assortment of tea sandwiches, dainty desserts and a steaming pot of tea in the center of their table. The rose decorated pot looked heavy, and so Irmajean did the honors then watched as Millicent daintily added two lumps of sugar and a lemon drop to her cup.

Tea fixed to her satisfaction, Millicent continued on. "Clarice's husband was an outsider and he brought changes to Rosewood." Millicent's mouth tightened as if she'd tasted something bitter.

"I've certainly never heard much about him." Which was true. Chalmers Carmichael's father was a mystery figure.

Millicent straightened her already straight shoulders. "He wasn't a gentleman. I've often wondered how he persuaded Clarice to marry him. She was used to a genteel way of life, even though she was a businesswoman and ran the paper after her father passed away. She was always a lady, and there was something coarse about Bertram Willowby. He smoked cigars, and his breath always smelled of whiskey."

Millicent hesitated and Irmajean felt she should respond. "It's hard to say what brings people together. How did they meet, do you know?"

"Clarice treated herself to a cruise for her thirty-fifth birthday. They met on board ship. The newspaper received a cable, which they published on the front page, that she had married a Bertram Willowby. The town, of course, was aghast since she had only been gone three weeks. People were eager to see the man who had won Clarice's heart, although there was considerable gossip that she had been offered and seized a last chance at matrimony."

Millicent nibbled a tomato sandwich and Irmajean poured her more tea and waited for the story to resume while the elderly novelist doctored her Earl Grey.

"Chalmers was born a year later, and although I hadn't been to the house since her marriage, I did feel I should take a small token of congratulations and see the baby." Her eyes took on a faraway look. "It seems strange that I've outlived not only Clarice, but her child. She adored Chalmers that was obvious. "But relations with Bertram were strained. The odor of his cigars was everywhere and when Clarice took me to see the baby, she confided that she and the child shared a suite on the second floor. There was always lots of gossip about Bertram Willowby, but I suppose that was because so many people didn't care for him. He was big and bluff, with slicked back dark hair. Still, Clarice as a wife not only came with money but with an assured social position, so people might talk, but he was never ostracized. And he did have his admirers."

"What kind of gossip?" Irmajean knew she'd hit pay dirt with Millicent.

Millicent was about to answer, when a surprise descended on their table in the form of Rose Campion. Multi-colored scarves fluttering and her magenta dirndl skirt flying, she eclipsed the impeccably and properly dressed Millicent, whose mouth tightened at sight of the flamboyant young woman with golden curls that formed an aura around her pert face. Irmajean sensed the temperature drop and feared Millicent's flow of information would now dry up. On the other hand, Irmajean not knowing Rose was alive and well and back in Pirate's Cove, was glad to see her.

"You're back!"

Rose Campion pulled out the third and empty chair and plunked herself down without invitation. "Irmajean, Millicent, I couldn't believe what happened while I was away." She showed no inclination to volunteer where she'd been.

Well, Irmajean thought, *you couldn't accuse Rose of being subtle.*

"Do they know who might have killed Priscilla?" Rose's mass of untamed curls seemed to grow even more electric as she talked, as if fueled by her energy.

Irmajean shook her head. "No, my understanding is that Frank Mallory is investigating a number of possibilities. She'd been going through some old records and boxes in the carriage house the day she was murdered, but whether or not that had anything to do with her death is anybody's guess."

Rose raised her eyebrows provocatively. "Maybe she stumbled upon a deadly secret."

Irmajean nodded, "Maybe."

"But you don't know anything more?"

" 'Fraid not."

"Perhaps the cards can tell us something." She pulled a well-used deck of Tarot cards from the pocket of her skirt.

Without asking, she moved the tiered tray still holding sandwiches and cakes to the side and began to shuffle the cards. Irmajean had wondered what it might be like to have her fortune told, but Rose's reading of the cards left her with the same feeling of generality that she had when reading her horoscope in the morning paper. Except for one piece of advice prefixed by a hard stare. "There is a trickster amongst us. Someone who is only playing a part." With that, she gathered up her cards and left with the same flourish with which she'd arrived.

All Irmajean could think of to say was, "Well!"

Millicent leaned forward and spoke in a low, conspiratorial tone. "I'm not sure she's the genuine article."

"I'm in agreement, but let's not give her another thought. I want to hear some more of your memories concerning Rosewood. I'm dying to know what the town was saying about Bertram Willowby."

"It was so long ago..."

"But the long ago is interesting. That's what makes your novels so fascinating—your grasp of the past and your skill in translating it into words." Irmajean hoped her flattery didn't sound too outlandish. Even though she didn't care much for Millicent's books, she had read a few of them, and they were well written and researched—if a bit improbable at times.

Millicent smiled and Irmajean saw her relax. "I try."

"Well, I would say you succeed admirably."

"Bertram was an abusive man. He was cruel in the things he said to people. He chided me about being unmarried and suggested perhaps I should take a cruise."

Irmajean choked on her tea and after much coughing managed to say, "That was rather a blatant jab at his own wife, wasn't it?"

"I can see that now, but at the time I was humiliated. Things weren't as easy then for a single woman as they are these days."

"Was he also physically abusive? Do you know?" Irmajean was uncertain whether any of this pertained in any way to Priscilla's murder, but you could never tell. In her own mind, she was becoming more and more convinced that something Priscilla had discovered about Rosewood had led to her death.

"I never saw him raise a hand to Clarice, but I did see him strike a Chinese servant who had been with Clarice's family for years. Shortly there after, the servant disappeared."

Irmajean felt prickles along her spine. "Was there any kind of an investigation?"

"If there was it was kept hush-hush. Word was given out that he'd left town. But it wasn't long after that, Clarice divorced Bertram. There were some who said she paid him to leave. I don't know if there was any truth in those stories or not. I do know that about this time Clarice began to practice stringent economies. Now whether she paid Bertram to divorce her or whether he ran through a good deal of her money I don't know."

"Wouldn't this have been during the Depression?"

Millicent nodded. "Yes, and so her economies might have been due to that. As people retired or quit the paper, she didn't fill their positions but took on their jobs herself. She closed up much of the house, let the gardeners go and became a recluse except when it came to work. One time I asked her why, and she said it was her penance for welcoming a viper into her nest."

"Which suggests she knew her husband well."

"Yes, but I asked her what she meant. Perhaps I was in hopes she would confide in me. But she simply said she was responsible for bringing evil to Pirate's Cove and until she had rooted it completely out, she couldn't have people at Rosewood."

"You say she let the gardens go. Is that when the hedge maze was neglected?"

"How do you know about that? I thought everyone had long ago forgotten about it? I know it's never mentioned."

Irmajean felt great satisfaction at this verbal confirmation. At last someone was owning up. "I ran across some newspaper clippings in Priscilla's office."

"Bertram was fascinated by the maze. Absolutely fascinated. He would disappear in there and be gone for hours according to Clarice. It seemed like in her mind the two became one. And so when she was rid of Bertram, she also wanted to be rid of the maze. But, of course, without gardeners, she couldn't have kept it up herself."

Irmajean refolded her linen napkin and laid it beside her empty plate. "Could you show me where the maze was? Do you remember?"

"Oh!" Millicent clearly hadn't expected such a request. "Well, yes, I suppose so. Although you could find it easily enough without me. It was just beyond the tea garden. That avenue of rose bushes led up to it."

Irmajean felt a tingle of excitement. "Directly to the entrance?"

Millicent nodded with assurance. "Yes." As if she anticipated Irmajean's next question she added, "I myself never went farther than just inside. There was always something frightening about it, and so I stayed away. But then most everyone stayed away once Bertram claimed it for his own."

"Most everyone?"

"Oh, he had his admirers. People he duped as he had originally fooled Clarice. Walter Meyers and Richard Lancaster were great friends of his, but then they, like Bertram, thought they were a cut above everyone else. They were men who truly believed they were superior because of their money and social position." Millicent thought a moment. "When I think how proud they all were of their family names it seems strange to me that none of their sons married and perpetuated the family lines."

"I've heard tell though that once upon a time they all loved the same woman. Do you know anything about that?"

Millicent nodded. "I remember her, yes. She was glamorous and exciting and she turned all the men in this town on their ear. She and the three bachelors became an inseparable foursome. I often wondered if she might not choose one of them and stay in Pirate's Cove, but I think we were too much of a small town, and she must have had her choice of dashing young men wherever she went." Irmajean noticed that this last was said somewhat wistfully.

"Tell me, Millicent. Did you ever think of leaving Pirate's Cove?"

"Plenty of times. But Mama needed me. My father hadn't left us very well off financially, and she came to depend on my teaching salary. I lived at home and so we were able to share living expenses. By the time Mama was gone and my writing was beginning to pay, I'd lost all desire to live anywhere else, although I have traveled. There are many wonderful places but this is home." She folded her napkin and pushed her chair a little away from the table. "I've enjoyed this immensely, Irmajean. You can't imagine how much. But I'm an old woman whether I want to admit it or not and I must rest every afternoon. Perhaps we could do this again sometime." A hopeful light gleamed in her eyes.

Irmajean was surprised how much she had enjoyed herself. "Not perhaps, but definitely."

They were about to part company when Millicent laid her gloved hand on Irmajean's arm. "Perhaps—until we know who harmed Priscilla, you would refrain from telling anyone the things I told you. I know they're ancient history, but some people have very long memories and I'd just as soon no one knew just how much I remember."

"Millicent, are you afraid of someone?"

Her laugh was artificial. "Of course not. Who could possibly mean me harm?"

That was exactly what Irmajean wondered as she watched the elderly novelist hurry away.

Thirteen

Irmajean, curious about Rose Campion's impromtu Tarot reading, decided to go in search of her. She ducked back inside the teashop, but Rose was nowhere in evidence. Irmajean intercepted one of the servers.

"Do you know where I can find Rose Campion?"

The girl hesitated, "You might try out back. I can't say for sure, but she sometimes sits in the back garden when she takes a break." Then the server added with an expression of regret. "They won't let you into the kitchen during business hours, so you'll have to enter from outside. Sorry."

Irmajean smiled her thanks and once more headed for the street. She knew she'd find access to the garden from a narrow alley that ran between the Cottage and the gift shop next door. Irmajean wrinkled her nose when it became evident that more than one dog—at least she hoped it was dogs—had made use of the alleyway. With profound relief, she spotted the gate leading into the back garden.

It was a charming tangle of rose bushes; shrub, floribunda, climbers, old-fashioned and hybrid tea. The air was positively euphoric and a welcome change from the odors of the alley. Irmajean filled her lungs and, for a moment, closed her eyes knowing one could get lost in this bower of blooms. When she again opened her eyes, it was to see that the garden was empty of any human presence but her own.

Taking a deep breath, she ducked into the alley and hurried as fast as she could to the street. It was there she collided with Barron Lancaster.

Clutching her hat, which had come askew in the collision, Irmajean looked up at the lawyer. Recovered from his momentary surprise, he frowned down at her. "What may I ask are you doing hanging about in alleys?" Then he sniffed audibly and wrinkled his nose.

All the disdain in the world was evident in his comment and his expression. Irmajean had no need to look down at her shoes to know what Lancaster smelled. It was even more evident to her that a souvenir of her foray through the alley clung to one or both of them. Well aware of how little Barron cared for her, she would not give him the satisfaction of glancing downward. Nevertheless, she couldn't help being a bit on the defensive. "I was looking for someone."

"In the alley?" His lip curled.

"It's the quickest way into the garden of the Cottage."

"There's access from the building."

"Not during business hours." She made no effort to keep the note of triumph from her voice. Barron was always so sure he knew more of everything than anybody else, that she made the most of knowing something he apparently didn't.

"I hope you found the alley pleasant." His expression was sly and Irmajean knew he hoped nothing of the sort. At the moment, she wished some dog would mistake his pant's leg for a fire hydrant.

"The garden was worth the short detour." On a whim she added, "I love roses. In fact, my next project at Rosewood is sprucing up the Rose Garden. There are several weddings booked there in the next few weeks, and I'd like to clear the area just beyond the rose path." His expression remained disinterested at best, so she added, "Who knows what lies at the end of the path?" She thought she saw a flicker of something in his eyes, perhaps annoyance. But whether or not it was annoyance at being detained or at what she said, Irmajean wasn't sure. She wouldn't want to play poker against his unreadable countenance.

"Isn't there enough garden as it is to keep you busy without your clearing more?"

She smiled sweetly, "Barron, don't you know by now that there can never be enough garden—anywhere. The busier the world gets, the more crowded, the more we're going to need oasis of nature."

His expression suggested that he thought her slightly mad. "Be careful, Irmajean, you don't get in over your head."

"Now am I likely to do that?" What she really wanted to say was, "Are you threatening me, Barron?"

"I think it possible, yes."

"And I think it the responsibility of the Friends of Rosewood to not only maintain the property but restore it to its former glory."

"Speaking of which, I'm calling a board meeting for tomorrow afternoon. There are some issues we need to discuss and the sooner the better."

"What time? I'll no doubt already be there, but in the garden somewhere."

"Should we say three o'clock?"

Irmajean nodded, "All right."

"I'll see you then."

She watched him stride down the street, shoulders erect, head high, thoughts perhaps on a time when to be a Lancaster really meant something. She wondered if he realized that those days were gone.

"Well, well, if it isn't the gardener from Rosewood."

With a start, Irmajean realized Karl Webster had come up behind her while her attention was on Barron Lancaster's retreating back. His California Poppy orange dreadlocks seemed charged with electricity and his eyes with mischief. Someone had once said to her that all the nuts seemed to roll to the coast and Karl gave justification to that remark. His hair alone made him a stand out in an area with more than its share of eccentrics.

Irmajean couldn't help grinning at Karl. "I've just been to tea with Millicent Morgan, and I happened to run into Barron Lancaster."

"Ah-h-h, yes, one of the Three. Chalmers Carmichael, Theodore Meyers, and Barron Lancaster. Once upon a time the most eligible bachelors in this fair town."

"So eligible that they spoiled on the vine?"

"I can see they haven't fooled you. But remember, not everything is as it seems."

"I couldn't agree with you more, Karl, but I do wonder what makes you think that things aren't as they seem?" Twice in the space of an hour she'd been warned of this.

"Because nothing is. Life is an illusion, and all we really experience is a reflection of reality."

"Plato?"

He neither confirmed nor denied her question, but shifted his weight from one leg to the other while lounging against the brick wall. "The benefits of a liberal arts education. Plus I like to read anything and everything."

"Did Priscilla ever allow you to borrow any of the books from Rosewood's library?"

"I wandered into the library one day when I'd stopped off to see Teddy. When she saw my interest was that of a scholar she let me read them, but I had to do so not only on the premises but in the library itself. She took her duties as protector of Rosewood seriously."

"Did she ever allow others the same privilege, do you know?"

"I know Jim Mills was after her to let him use some of the books in his history class, but she was pretty adamant in telling him no. I don't think she trusted ole Jimmy."

"Smart girl." She knew Jim had been lying.

She bid Karl good-bye and trotted down the street, muttering to herself as she went that there were too many loose ends and too many unanswered questions. So engrossed was she in this obvious conclusion that she was to the end of the block before remembering that she had intended to run Rose Campion to ground. Turning on her heel, she hurried back to the tearoom. The room was now empty except for the same young woman she'd talked to earlier.

She glanced up from setting the tables and smiled when she recognized Irmajean. "Hi, did you find Rose?"

"No, no, I didn't. I ran into some other people I knew however."

"Yeah, I saw you talking to Rose's boyfriend."

"Rose's boyfriend?"

"Yeah, the guy with the orange dreadlocks. He often meets Rose in the garden."

"How interesting." How right he was when he said nothing was as it seemed. "Is Rose still here?"

"Oh, I'm sorry. She left just a few minutes ago. Can I tell her you were looking for her?"

"No, that's all right. I'll be seeing her tomorrow anyway. But thanks."

Rose and Karl both had warned her someone wasn't who they seemed. Was it just a general warning or did they have someone specific in mind?

Fourteen

While filling the teakettle with water, Irmajean caught a glimpse of herself in the kitchen window. Darkness reigned outside, it was after all two o'clock in the morning, and so she saw only her own reflection. It wasn't a pretty sight since the area around her eyes was puffy, which made her eyes look like two raisins stuck in dough. Besides that, her hair was at sixes and sevens. "I'd turn Medusa to stone," she muttered.

While the water heated, she rummaged in the toffee tin cum tea canister that had been her grandmother's until she found a peppermint tea bag. Smokey jumped up onto the counter. "You know you're not allowed up here." But neither woman nor cat did anything about it, and so the fluffy gray feline continued to watch with a wisdom-of-the-ages expression in her wide green eyes.

Irmajean liked her tea stout and while she waited for it to steep, she stroked Smokey and reflected there was nothing she could think of more soothing than a cup of tea and the company of a fine cat. While sipping her tea she heard the stairs creak and the shuffle, shuffle of her husband's feet. "I didn't mean to wake you."

"Is there enough water for me to have a cup of something?"

"Certainly." She set about making him a cup of Chamomile. "There's even a cookie left."

"No, I've had my share. Those are yours. Do you need to talk?"

Irmajean, her mouth full of cookie, nodded.

"Can we sit down while we do it?"

She nodded again and carried her cup to the table where she sat down opposite her blurry-eyed husband. "We're a pair," she thought. "Approaching our sixties and comfortable with each other as a pair of old slippers. Not at all glamorous, but definitely happy."

"Still troubling over Priscilla?"

She cupped her hands around her steaming mug and nodded. "I keep thinking we're overlooking something. Something important. I've tried to let go of it. To tell myself that Frank Mallory is more than capable and will get to a solution eventually."

"I'm sure he will."

"But he hasn't said as much. Wouldn't he let us know if he was on to something?"

"Why should he, Irmajean? Because we're friends?"

She shrugged. "There's that, but mainly because I'm involved with Rosewood and because, well, because I care."

She wasn't fooling him for a minute. "And because you're bound and determined to poke your nose into the whole affair." He rested his arms on the table and nailed her attention with a serious expression. "Do you ever stop to consider you might be getting too close to whatever got Priscilla killed?"

"If I knew anything I might. But so far I don't know a darned thing!"

Irmajean was thoughtful while she sipped her cooling tea. "You know, I hate to think someone I know, trust, work with could be guilty of murder. But if Priscilla was killed because of something she'd found then it seems a given at least one of the Rosewood Board of Directors is responsible."

"You've mentioned more than once that she didn't always see eye to eye with all of them."

"I think I understood her better than any of the other board members because she is—was about the same age as our girls. Some of the others just threw up their hands in despair when she'd dig her heels in over some issue. Here were Ted and Barron, two old bachelors. I doubt either of them ever understood a woman in their life or even wanted to. There's no refuge in understanding. Then there is Jim Mills who cozied up to her, but probably only for his own ends. Frederick, I believe, is basically afraid of women. Perhaps he has enough trouble keeping his life on track without complicating it with relationships. Besides, there's his dog. Who could ask for a more faithful companion?"

"How did Frederick end up here? Do you have any idea? Do you even know where he came from?" By now, Glenn had warmed to their discussion.

"He never says much about himself or anyone else, for that matter. I suppose like so many people he drove through, liked what he saw and decided to stay awhile. All I know for certain is that he's done a lot of invaluable restoration carpentry at Rosewood. Repairs we would had to have postponed if he hadn't done the work *gratis*. Besides that, he's the best. Wood responds to him, and he's passionate about preserving and restoring Rosewood."

"Would you say he might be a little bit obsessed with the house?"

"No more than I am about the gardens."

"Okay, so who does that leave?"

"There's Millicent who at eighty-two really isn't a strong contender for the role of murderer. Priscilla's death involved a great deal of physical strength, which I think is beyond her as it is Ted and Barron. And Frederick would jump off the roof before he'd put a hole in Rosewood."

"So is that it?"

Irmajean shook her head. "No, I'm forgetting Tess Brock. But I can't see her killing Priscilla—unless there was a buck to be made from it. Which isn't a very nice thing to say..."

"But nevertheless the truth." As a real estate appraiser, Honey had had more than one opportunity to lock horns with Tess.

"However, she doesn't care in the least what anyone thinks of her. I doubt Priscilla could have found anything that would have bothered Tess. That leaves Rose Campion. And I can't think of a single reason why Rose would kill Priscilla."

"Except you've told me more than once you don't think Rose Campion is her real name."

"Well, I don't think it is. I don't think she's real, for that matter."

"What do you mean by that?"

Irmajean took a deep breath and thought how to explain what she did mean. "She's a little much. As if she was trying hard to be different and eccentric and woo-woo and..."

"Just a minute. What do you mean by woo-woo?"

"New Agey. Metaphysical. Some people just are. Others try. I think Rose Campion is one of those who are trying. And she's trying a little too hard." She leaned forward and without realizing it, dropped her voice. "While Millicent and I were having tea, Rose did a spread of Tarot cards for us. The reading was pretty general, until she looked me right in the eye and said someone wasn't who they seemed. A comment I would have dismissed if she hadn't given me such a knowing look when she said it."

"You think she knows something?"

"I don't know if she does or not. But within the hour I ran into Karl Webster, and he told me the same thing. Then I found out he and Rose are dating."

"Maybe they're just pulling your leg."

"Maybe, but what if they're not?"

They sat in silence for a few minutes. Both lost in thought and trying to make sense of everything they'd been discussing. Finally Irmajean sighed. "How do we get to the truth?"

"*We* don't. *We* let Frank Mallory earn the money the taxpayers are paying him. Now, I'm going back to bed."

"I'll be there in a minute." But it was more than ten minutes before she climbed the stairs to join her husband.

Irmajean was up and ready early in the morning. She had a lot to do before the board meeting, and she knew how quickly time could get away from her. She liked being at Rosewood early in the morning when the grass was still damp and everything smelled fresh. New buds would just be opening while old ones would be renewed by the coolness of night. Everyday there were changes in the garden and surprises. Sometimes a plant she'd all but given up on would decide to bloom. And while it might sound silly to a non-gardener, such a happening always brought a leap of joy into her heart.

Besides, she was in hopes that by arriving early at Rosewood she might renew the connection she'd always felt with the venerable old house. Priscilla's murder had not only removed Rosewood's director, but it had eliminated the ease with which Irmajean moved around the property. An uninvited guest had taken up residence at Rosewood, moving silently through the narrow hallways and turning up in the most unlikely places. This shadow of doubt was not a comfortable companion, and it took liberties no well-behaved guest should take. Last night or rather in the wee small hours of the morning, Irmajean had resolved that the shadow of doubt would be a short-term guest. For Priscilla's sake, for Rosewood's sake, but perhaps most of all for her own.

The morning was cool, although all the signs promised a glorious day. Even though the ocean was a mere two miles away, Rosewood's location nestled against the foothills of the Coast Range sheltered it from the cool winds that could blow along the beach. On a day like this, it could get darned hot by afternoon.

Early as she was, Ted was there before her and also Frederick Blumer. She parked beside his truck, being careful to leave the windows down on her car so it wouldn't be like crawling into an oven when it was time to go home. Taking her garden gloves and her hat from the seat, she stopped long enough to pat Frederick's faithful dog, Goblin, who lolled in the back of his truck. He'd explained to her once that he'd derived the dog's name from a favorite poem *Little Orphant Annie* by James Whitcomb Riley. The Newfoundland was always glad to see her; always glad to see everyone for that matter. Then she started down the various winding paths that would eventually take her to the rose garden. A tough little pair of garden clippers sagged in her pocket along with other odds and ends.

It was a perfect May morning, and the roses were just coming into their own with blooms of every color. She stopped to admire the variegated beauty of Betty Boop, a charmer in the garden and long lasting in bouquets. The colorful roses might have been a rainbow fallen from the sky. Now it seemed she might find a treasure at the end of this particular rainbow. Millicent claimed the entrance to the hedge maze was at the end of the rose path. Irmajean was determined to find it. Clamping her hat on her head and pulling her gloves on her hands, she took her clippers from her pocket and set to work on a tangled crop of blackberry vines.

Millicent's memory placed the entrance to the maze at the end of the path between the roses. So Irmajean concentrated on a five-foot area in that general vicinity. She'd been snipping away at blackberries for what seemed hours but was probably only fifteen minutes when she stopped for a rest. When it came to garden work she was in pretty good shape, but thinking about clearing the supposed entrance to the maze and actually doing it were two different things. Besides blackberries were a tough adversary. Her arms were already tired and scratched and while she'd created an impressive pile of debris, as far as she could tell she'd made no headway towards her goal. Could Millicent have remembered wrong?

Knee high grass grew up around the base of the blackberries and she wondered if parting it and trying to look under the barrier rather than hacking through it would do any good. To that purpose, she deposited her clippers in her pocket and got down on her hands and knees. Patting the grass down as she crawled, she accomplished nothing other than to look foolish should anyone be watching.

Still on her hands and knees, she thought she heard something moving in the brush. Holding her breath she listened, heard nothing more and was about to blame her imagination when something rustled the shrubbery. Almost immediately, two glowing eyes looked directly into hers. With a yelp and an agility that surprised her almost more than anything, Irmajean sprang to her feet. The noise she made startled whatever had startled her, and she heard it retreat into the brush, following a route she could only guess at. But it distracted her enough that she heard nothing else until it was too late. Not even her faithful garden hat could deflect the blow to the back of her head that sent her sprawling in a very undignified manner amongst the blackberries.

Fifteen

Much later Irmajean would deny that she'd ever lost consciousness entirely, but even she wasn't sure if that was fact or wishful thinking. She distinctly remembered someone dragging her through the brush. She'd wanted to open her eyes, but a two-fold sense of self-preservation prevented her. She wanted to protect her eyes from the berry bushes that were slashing at her mercilessly. And much as she wanted to identify her assailant, she didn't want to risk giving away the fact that she was still aware of what was going on around her. When several minutes had passed and she was no longer being moved about like a sack of fertilizer, she carefully opened her eyes.

Greenery towered above her, tangled and overgrown. Where there wasn't green, there was blue sky with gently whirling white clouds. The tops of the shrubbery also seemed to be whirling. Irmajean closed her eyes again, took a deep breath, and again opened them. The heavens seemed to have settled down a bit and so she risked trying to sit up. A mistake, she realized, when she was almost overwhelmed with nausea. Her head felt as if it were being pummeled with croquet mallets.

For a while longer, she lay in the sweet smelling grass glad that it was a warm day and not wet. She told herself she'd feel better soon, and then she could find her way out of the garden to the house and a telephone. She wasn't exactly certain where she was, but felt confident once her head cleared all questions would be answered. Eyes closed, she enjoyed the warmth of the sun until a sudden weight settled on her chest. Her eyes flew open to see Catkin bearing gifts. A tiny mouse dangled from his mouth. When he saw she was awake, he dropped it on her chest, only to have the mouse quickly regain consciousness and run. With a narrowing of his eyes, Catkin was off in pursuit.

Irmajean raised her hand to the back of her head and it came away a bit sticky. Well, wasn't a little blood to be expected when someone smashed you on the head? A subsequent examination of the rest of her revealed no other wounds other than those inflicted by the blackberry bushes. But it also revealed that somewhere she'd lost her hat. She hadn't seen it coming; hadn't a clue who it might have been. Since she was no lightweight, it seemed safe to assume that her attacker had been a man. Or if not a man an incredibly strong woman. Catkin returned, emerging from a small tunnel in the brush.

"Well, you're a welcome sight." He purred as if to confirm her statement. "Can you tell me where I am? Better yet, can you tell me how to get out?"

At this, he jumped from her lap and headed back the way he'd come.

"Wait!" And Irmajean got painfully to her knees and tried crawling in Catkin's direction. He tunneled through the grass and underbrush, either following a path of his own making or one carved by woodland creatures. Because she saw at a glance that it was well-traveled. But well-traveled enough for her to wriggle through? There was only one way to find out. She put her hand down and immediately felt something cool and wiggly. Looking down she locked gazes with the beady eyes of a garter snake. Giving a startled gasp, she pulled back, got her hair tangled on a branch and lost sight of Catkin. When she finally untangled herself and crawled through the tunnel, it was to find herself on an overgrown, yet barely discernable path.

Rising unsteadily to her feet with the help of a shrub and standing with her eyes closed for a moment while the world settled into place, Irmajean thought she knew where she was. Awful as she felt, she also felt a rising excitement. She was in the garden maze. Had to be. Yew, long untrimmed, grew either side of where she stood. She could see it made a sharp turn not far ahead.

So what did she do now? And why had her attacker brought her here? Had they hoped she'd languish, die and never be found? Irmajean told herself it was a ridiculous notion, while at the same time trying not to think that mazes were designed to confound, and this one had the added benefit of being overgrown. The blow to her head had left her feeling a bit muddled and even though she turned full circle, she could identify no familiar point of reference.

If only she was feeling a little more herself then she could enjoy the thrill of knowing the hedge maze at Rosewood was a reality. While grateful the attack on her was no more serious, she could also wonder why not? Had it been meant as only a warning? Regardless, it left her feeling in a bit of a panic. She had to find her way out of the maze. Thinking, something she'd always been very good at, was extremely difficult at the moment. She had no idea which way to go, but she knew she couldn't just stand there. Glancing up at the sun, she wondered should she follow its progression to freedom? The house was located southwest of where she'd been working, so could she work her way out of the maze by following the direction of the sun as it moved westward? It seemed logical, but what was she to do with herself while she waited for the day to wane? She certainly couldn't sit, stand, or do nothing. Perhaps it wouldn't hurt to *try* to find her way out.

She would mark her trail with strips of twine from the roll in her pocket. That way she'd know it if she doubled back on herself. The original hedge plantings were dense and impenetrable, which was a good thing because that kept her to the intended path. As she stumbled along, snipping here, tying a piece of twine there, she felt quite in sympathy with Theseus. They both faced the unknown twists and turns of a labyrinth, unsure what lay around the next corner. In her case, she hoped nothing as deadly as a Minotaur—or a dangerous and determined killer.

Sixteen

Irmajean wandered the maze first with enthusiasm and then, after a while, like a lost sheep. Her head hurt, she was occasionally overcome with dizziness and nausea, and, once in a while, with a confusion she couldn't quite understand. Then the fear would arise that perhaps some serious harm had been done to her head, and that she would wander interminably between the untrimmed rows of privet and yew. After awhile she began to feel hungry and took that as a good sign. It was further good news when Catkin rounded a corner and strolled toward her.

She stooped to pick him up and almost lost her balance when her head swam alarmingly. "Nice, Catkin. Can you show me the way out? Please?" She put the cat down and watched as he retraced his route of only moments before. As long as he didn't disappear into the shrubbery she could follow him, even though he didn't take the avenues that she would have selected left on her own. In a matter of minutes, Irmajean found herself standing in the heart of the maze. Here there was a small gazebo covered in tangled vines with stone benches on two sides and in the center a statue of Atlas holding the world.

"Well," she told Catkin. "At least I have somewhere to sit besides the ground." The gazebo was charming, and she could imagine glasses and a pitcher of lemonade awaiting tired pilgrims who reached the center of the maze. Although reaching the center was only solving half the puzzle, there was still the necessity of finding her way out. Unfortunately, the thought of lemonade made her aware how thirsty she was and how hot and muggy the day had become. The sun overhead was warm and the hedge blocked any breeze that might have been. The gazebo, however, was shady, and she sat down with a grateful sigh and closed her eyes. After a few moments of blissful rest, she forced her eyes open, stared at the pedestal of the statue and frowned.

It took more energy than Irmajean thought she had left, nevertheless she exerted herself to rise and walk over to the cracked and weary Atlas. He should have sat square in the center of the gazebo and from a standing position it appeared he did. But from her vantage point on the bench, she had noticed a small space along the bottom edge of the pedestal. Was there some kind of opening beneath it? Probably not, but she was insatiably curious even at the worst of times. And while this wasn't the worst of times, it definitely qualified in the runner-up category.

Irmajean picked up a skinny stick, got down on her knees and leaning against the statue poked the stick in what appeared to be a small opening. She hadn't known what to expect, but it certainly wasn't for the statue to move as she leaned her weight against it. But move it did, albeit with much scraping and grinding, to reveal a square opening and several steps that disappeared into the

darkness. Her heart thumped with excitement at the
possibilities of what she'd found. It took no imagination to
think she'd located the entrance to a tunnel, but where did
it lead? She was reminded that Frederick had suggested
only days ago that he suspected such a tunnel wandered
beneath the grounds of Rosewood.

Irmajean could hardly contain her curiosity as she
peered into the dark opening once guarded by a weary
Atlas. If only she carried a flashlight in her pocket instead
of a pair of clippers. On her hands and knees, she stuck
her head into the opening and was greeted with the
pungent smell of damp earth. Where did the steps lead?
Raising herself to a sitting position, she realized there was
nothing she could do now but wonder. Later, when she
had found her way out of the maze she would bring
Honey back with a flashlight. Together, they would
explore where the steps went, where the tunnel led. But
she certainly wasn't going to wander around underground
in the dark. Her sense of adventure wasn't that great.
Besides, what if the person who had knocked her
senseless watched her even now? If she were to disappear
underground there would be nothing to stop them from
pushing Atlas back in position. And she wasn't at all
certain she could move him if she were underneath. That
thought was as unnerving as the one that her attacker
might be watching her at this very moment. Watching and
waiting and perhaps poised to strike—again.

Catkin, who had obviously been on a hunting safari,
returned to investigate what she was doing, laying his
mouse aside for future consideration and venturing into
the hole. Quickly he descended the steps and, without

thinking, she reached for him in an attempt to stop him. But while the cat whisked out of her reach, her hand did brush something that felt like a cord. It might simply be a root, but she had to know and steeled herself to reach once again into the unknown. Within seconds her fingers surrounded what definitely felt like a cord or a string. Not considering any possible consequences, she tugged on it and was more surprised than ever to have a light flicker on.

Without a second thought, Irmajean descended into the tunnel. A row of light bulbs stretched along the ceiling and provided a weak illumination that dimmed alarmingly and then brightened again. The obvious fact that the tunnel had been wired for electricity suggested to Irmajean that it had been in frequent use—at least at one time. Irmajean progressed cautiously. She'd never heard a single hint or rumor of this underground passageway beyond Frederick Blumer's speculations. Which suggested a clandestine purpose or had the tunnel been constructed for the convenience of the servants who would have to supply weary maze wanderers with refreshments? It seemed logical to assume the tunnel would connect with the house. And as it was uncluttered and seemed to run in a fairly straight line she felt she could find her way back to the steps even if—God forbid—the lights failed.

Unlike the maze, the tunnel took no twists or turns. Whatever its original purpose, it wasn't to confound. It was well constructed, the floor paved with bricks and precautions taken to prevent cave-ins. But there were still more surprises in store when she came upon a circular

room with a mosaic floor, stone benches and a lectern
which held a slim ledger style book. Over to the side stood
what seemed to be a large wardrobe. The whole
appearance was that of a meeting room. But a meeting
room for what and why underground? Would anything
positive be conducted in such a place? She shivered and
hugged herself. A miasma of unpleasantness seemed to
linger that she couldn't blame on her imagination. Had
this underground lair been the work of Bertram
Willowby? Millicent claimed he was not a nice man.
What had happened to him and the missing servant? In
this earthen place, it was possible to conjure up anything,
and she felt an absurd desire to run away. But she had
little choice of places to go. The tunnel stretched into a
flickering darkness and, while she watched, one of two
remaining bulbs winked out.

She hesitated, wondering if she could continue seeing
anything. The pain in her head had settled down to a dull
throb, but she still had to swallow occasionally against
bouts of nausea. *Still*, she asked herself, *what harm could
there be in continuing on—cautiously?* Especially if the
way did lead back to Rosewood. Each step was tentative
and accompanied by outstretched arms. The passage
seemed never-ending, but when it did she bumped into a
solid wall.

She warned herself not to panic, but it was easier said
than done. Much easier. This couldn't be a dead end. She
ran her hands over the walls. Was this really a skillfully
hidden door with a latch she might trip if only she could
find it? She felt the gauziness of spider webs beneath her
fingers and tried not to think what might lurk unseen. But

all her searching yielded nothing. There had to be some way into that underground meeting room other than through the hedge maze. Access from the house seemed logical. According to Millicent, something unfortunate had occurred at Rosewood. Had that unfortunate something caused Clarice Carmichael to seal access to the tunnel?

Irmajean was about to give up and retrace her steps when she heard the sound of pounding and a muffled murmur of voices. *Of course!* The Board of Directors meeting was going on at that very moment. Which meant—given the early hour in which she'd arrived at Rosewood—that a great deal of time had passed almost unnoticed. Could she make anyone hear her? She decided it was darn well worth a try and she began to pound and call out as loudly as she could. "Hello, can you hear me? Hello, it's Irmajean. I need help." She hollered until her throat felt raw and pounded until her hands throbbed.

Seventeen

Barron Lancaster banged the gavel and waited for the gaggle of board members to come to attention and realize he was in charge. His eyes scanned those present and he saw everyone was there save one. "Has anyone seen Irmajean today?"

Everyone in the room exchanged looks, and one by one shook their heads. Millicent hesitantly raised her hand. "Did she know about the meeting? She didn't say anything about it when I saw her yesterday."

Barron nodded. "She knew. I told her myself. It's not like her to be absent without telling someone."

"You look a little worried, Barron. Is there a reason for that?" Tess Brock spoke without asking to be recognized.

He glared at Tess. "I'd be concerned at the unexplained absence of any of you, considering there's still a killer on the loose. Or have you all forgotten so soon?"

Tess took exception to his tone. "I don't think we've forgotten at all. Especially as *some*_of us were quite fond of Priscilla. But Irmajean is a sensible woman. I suspect she's in the garden somewhere, happily unaware that it's time for this command appearance of the Rosewood board of directors."

Someone snickered and Barron glared. Ted adjusted his glasses and cleared his throat. "I move we get started. I can fill Irmajean in on whatever we discuss as well as give her a copy of the minutes." He sat at attention, pen in hand, unblemished notepad before him.

"Very well, then. Let's get on with it. In the absence of a director, I'll head up the discussion. Ted, please record that the meeting was called to order and who was in attendance. The main subject up for discussion is who will take responsibility for Rosewood while we search for a new director. Also, do we want to hire someone full time or only part time? Or do we want to rely on volunteers? I'll take suggestions from the floor."

Millicent hesitantly raised her hand. "Isn't it just the littlest bit unseemly to be discussing a replacement for Priscilla when—when…"

Tess finished for her. "When not only isn't she even cold in her grave, but she isn't even in it."

Barron drew himself up stiffly. "Tragic as the loss of Priscilla is, we can't put the running of Rosewood on hold indefinitely. There are programs in the works and decisions to be made. If we're going to survive then we need to move forward."

Rose Campion was next to risk a suggestion. "I think we should offer the directorship to Irmajean. Nobody cares more about this place than she does. She could navigate the garden with her eyes closed and is here practically every day anyway. Besides, she and Priscilla were close. If anyone can know what our late director had in mind for Rosewood it would probably be Irmajean."

Jim Mills jumped to his feet. "If she takes over as director I'll resign from the board. She already acts like she owns this place."

Rose turned on him with a flash of anger. "Jim Mills, you know that isn't true! You're only mad at her because she wouldn't let you rob the library."

Bad news and gossip travel quickly in a small town, and they all knew he'd almost gotten away with the valuable Chinook jargon dictionary. Quick action on Irmajean's part and quick response on the part of the police had intercepted Jim and the dictionary before he had a chance to sell it.

Jim turned red in the face, sputtered and then sat down.

Tess gave him a lopsided smile. "It's hard to keep a secret in a town this size, Jim boy. You might want to bear that in mind the next time you head south to the casino."

Ted again cleared his throat. "As secretary-treasurer for Rosewood may I say a few words?" As nobody dissented, he continued on. "The truth is, our funds are rather low. When we hired Miss Norris we agreed to pay her what I considered to be a ridiculously high salary." He raised a hand to silence a sudden grumbling. "I won't say she wasn't worth it." Although he had more than once suggested as much, but that was water under the bridge. And one really shouldn't speak ill of the dead. "But I will state, and the financial figures agree with me, that we can't afford to pay anyone what we paid her or we'll be bankrupt in a year's time. In fact, even Priscilla realized what a drain her salary was on Rosewood. She'd volunteered to take a cut in salary just days before..." He swallowed and cleared his throat. "What I would suggest is that we continue with the fund raisers Priscilla had set in motion, particularly the garden events that Irmajean has already agreed to oversee, and that we each agree to spend some volunteer time in the office. Then perhaps at the end of another year, we will be in a position to again hire someone at least part time."

"You could sell off some of that library and have plenty of operating capital." This from a disgruntled Jim Mills.

Ted jumped to his feet. "No! The library must remain intact. The books are valuable."

Mills almost snarled. "That's my point."

Tess glanced his way. "You should know that better than anyone, huh, Jim boy." His temper flared. "Like you would know. When was the last time you even read a book?"

She smiled at him knowingly. "Unlike some people, my tastes are a bit more cerebral than a betting/racing book."

Barron banged the gavel repeatedly and suddenly the head flew off and skittered across the table just as Jim Mills lunged toward Tess. Frederick Blumer caught a hold of his arm and pushed him back into his chair. His interference gave Barron the opportunity to regain control of the meeting if not the gavel.

"If we're going to waste time name calling and exchanging insults we never will reach a decision.

Again Millicent raised her hand, and he nodded in her direction. "Perhaps we could charge a nominal fee for people to use the library. First, we'd have to make it known that we have considerable research materials."

Mills sneered at the old woman. "Yeah, like that's gonna bring in the big bucks."

Millicent flushed and blinked rapidly. "It was only a suggestion. I know myself I've had to pay for the privilege of using certain research materials."

Rose Campion came to the elderly novelist's defense. "That's a great idea. No, it probably wouldn't bring in a lot of revenue. But I think we have to make use of every possible means we can if Rosewood is going to survive as it is now."

Millicent smiled her appreciation and was sorry she'd suggested to Irmajean only yesterday that she wondered if Rose knew her Tarot cards as well as she should.

Barron tapped what remained of his gavel. "I appreciate these fund raising suggestions and think they should be implemented, but we've strayed from the subject at hand. What do we do about a director?"

Tess got to her feet. "I think a final decision on that score should be left until Irmajean can be polled. Either that or a decision hinge on her approval, because she and Ted spend the most time here." Forestalling any objections, she continued on. "However if they both agree, I move that we continue for a few months on a volunteer basis. I could give a few hours a week, and I'd venture to say I'm as busy as any of you. I'd like to see Rosewood make it, she's a grand old dame of a house."

Frederick Blumer stood up. "I second Tess's motion. We could replace the present phone with a cordless one. Most people call before coming out. I could make some signs that say, *In the Garden* or *In the Carriage House*. Then those of us who donate our hands-on-expertise could use our volunteer time to good advantage while having the telephone at hand. Rosewood must be preserved and maintained at all costs."

Barron, relieved to have a decision reached, called for a vote. "All in favor raise their hands." The vote was unanimous except for Jim Mills who was apparently abstaining. "Jim, how do you vote?"

Mills shoved his chair back from the table. "I don't vote. I resign. This place is an albatross, but you all refuse to see it. You keep thinking the band aid approach will save it, when all it'll do is postpone the inevitable." They sat in silence while he stalked from the room and slammed the door behind him. Then you could almost hear a collective sigh of relief.

Tess was the first one to actually give her verbal approval to his departure. "Now at least we won't have to keep the books under lock and key."

Ted cleared his throat. "Actually that might not be such a bad idea." Millicent raised her hand and waited for Barron to acknowledge her. "I've been thinking about those books, and I think I know which ones you're referring to. We might want to consider raising the money to have them reprinted. Those anyway where the copyright has expired. It would be a wonderful way to raise money."

Tess turned toward her. "But wouldn't it cost a lot to have them published?"

Millicent was about to respond when a muffled knocking came from within the entryway wall and startled them all into silence. For once, Millicent threw shyness to the winds. "I hear something. Something coming from the entry. From beneath the stairs." She knocked over her chair as she hurried from the room, dropping an immaculate glove in the process. The others followed her and formed a loose cluster staring at the wood paneling beneath the stairs.

Tess turned to Frederick Blumer. "Do you have a pry bar in your truck? Something we can use to remove that wall?"

Not much of his face was visible beneath his beard, but what they could see paled. "You can't destroy that paneling!"

Tess turned on him. "Oh, for God's sake, Frederick. Somebody might be trapped in there and getting them out is a lot more important than any damned paneling."

Rose Campion hovered beside Millicent who had her ear to the wall. "Perhaps it's a ghost. I've always thought this house felt haunted." She had her mouth open to say more when Millicent shushed her.

"I can't hear if you're all talking." When they fell silent, she rapped her knuckles hard against the glossy wood.

~ * ~

Irmajean could have cried with relief when she heard the faint knocking. Someone, bless their soul, had heard her. "It's Irmajean. Help me, please." And she pounded as hard as she could on the wall.

~ * ~

Her eyes wide with wonder, Millicent glanced round the semicircle of board members. "It's Irmajean. How in the world did she ever get on the other side of this wall?"

Tess didn't venture a guess, but she did issue an ultimatum. "Frederick, either you open this wall or I will and I can guarantee given the circumstances that I don't give a damn what happens to this paneling. You at least might be able to save it."

"Okay, Okay. I'll get something from my truck." If he'd been a kettle, he'd have been steaming.

"Well, don't take forever," Tess called to his retreating back.

There was nothing they could do but wait. Millicent spent the time uttering encouraging words to Irmajean that the rest of them doubted she could hear, but who were they to say. Anyway, Tess was more interested in why Barron and Ted had their heads together.

Barron, a good deal taller than Ted, placed himself between his oldest surviving friend and the rest of the Rosewood board members. He hoped if any of the others had seen Ted wringing his hands they thought it was simply because of concern for Irmajean. Only Barron could know differently. He spoke in a low hiss when he chided the smaller man. "For God's sake, get a grip on yourself! You'll give us both away if you don't."

"How could she have found the tunnel?" The words came out as a croak.

"Who knows how that meddlesome old biddy does anything?" Barron was trying not to let Ted know how concerned he was over Irmajean Lloyd's obvious and unfortunate discovery.

"She'll find everything. She'll know and she'll tell everyone. We'll be ruined." The words came out almost as a wail.

"Sh-h-h, or someone will hear you, and Irmajean won't have to tell anybody anything because you'll already have done it."

"But how could she have gotten in there?" Ted echoed his thoughts.

"Listen," he hissed. "I don't want to discuss this further until we can be certain we're alone. She must have somehow discovered the entrance to the tunnel." Something he had never expected. "The important thing is not to panic."

Ted was trembling both inside and out. He knew they would be found out. He'd always known it, and the possibility had lurked in the background of his life—coloring it, shaping it, tainting it. Gone would be their good names and their place in the community. He felt like he was going to be sick and hurried quickly to the bathroom while Barron waited for Frederick to return and open the wall.

Once there had been a door with a hidden spring. Quite clever really. But he was not about to reveal his knowledge of it. And perhaps Clarice had taken care of it. Several years older than Chalmers, he remembered well the day she'd discovered what had been going on in that underground chamber. Bertram had thought himself quite the man, but he'd been no match for the enraged and appalled Clarice.

Frederick Blumer returned with his toolbox, moved the tall basket containing Pampas Grass and began trying to open the wall without damaging the paneling.

Tess stood there tapping her foot. "Frederick, there is a human being on the other side of that wall. One we're all acquainted with, so maybe you could hurry it up a bit."

"I don't want to ruin the paneling. With just a little bit of care I can save it." When the section of wall came loose, it did so with surprising ease, and he could see that it had been so well designed to fit into place that no nails or anything had been used. But when it was removed a solid wall was revealed. The group let out a collective groan.

Tess was quick to take charge. "I don't think we need to preserve this inner wall. Just knock it down."

"But it's part of history. Part of this grand old house." Sweat beaded Frederick Blumer's brow.

"Frederick, if you don't knock that wall down pronto then I will, and you'd better stand out of the way." Tess couldn't believe Frederick's obstinacy. "What if Irmajean runs out of air?"

Frederick gave her a look that suggested he found that darned unlikely, while Barron looked on if they dared hope that might happen. Then Frederick took a claw hammer out of his toolbox and started prying boards loose.

Irmajean heard all the activity on the other side and knew someone was doing something to help her. She didn't mean to be ungrateful, but she certainly hoped it wasn't the person who had knocked her over the head. Something furry rubbed against her and she gave a little yelp, then felt foolish when she heard a meow. "Catkin, is that you?" At that moment, a section of boards came loose and she blinked in the sudden light. Catkin jumped up and through the opening, surprising Frederick who was preparing to tear some more boards free.

"No, it's me, Irmajean." Now that the end of her ordeal was in sight, the darkness was becoming oppressive and the panic she'd fought so successfully up until now began to assert itself. "Please, could you maybe hurry! I'd like to get out of here."

Tess bent down and called through the cat-sized opening Frederick had already created. "Hang on, Irmajean. We'll get you out of there. Then you sure as heck have you some explaining to do." She was about to start in on some of the boards herself, then remembered she'd had her nails done just that morning. "Come on, Frederick. Let's get with it."

He seemed to pay her no mind, but Millicent, ever observant of the kind of details that gave life to her stories, thought he exerted a little too much force on the next board he pulled from the wall. Perhaps that was why it snapped in his huge hands.

When the wall was dismantled enough for Irmajean to climb through, they were all stunned into silence. From the expressions on their faces, she knew she looked as bad, maybe even worse, than she felt. For a moment no one spoke, and then everyone started talking, the words tumbling around her as unintelligible scrapes of sound. Barron Lancaster had almost been speechless at the sight of her, but his years as a courtroom lawyer stood him in good stead. Recovering quickly, he once more gained control of the meeting. He was, after all, chairman of the Rosewood Board of Directors. He strode over to Irmajean. Dear God, the woman looked more disheveled than usual, and putting his arm around her—a solicitous performance that should have earned him an award—lead her to the softest chair in the living room.

Irmajean, astute if she was anything, looked sideways at him with narrowed eyes. She was well aware what Barron Lancaster thought of her and this sudden show of solicitousness was totally out of character. If he'd been alone in the house when she started pounding on the wall, she would have expected him to walk out the door, turning off the lights as he went. So she wasn't impressed by his current behavior, just suspicious. She was tempted to lean heavily against him—cobwebs, dirt and all—and wail piteously, just to see what he would do. However, she didn't. Rather, she took a deep breath and said instead, "Would someone mind fixing me a cup of tea?"

It was Ted, recovered from his earlier distress, who hastened into the kitchen. She couldn't ever recall seeing him respond so quickly to any emergency, real or imagined. He was usually too busy wringing his hands. Today that task fell to Millicent.

"Oh, Irmajean, whatever happened to you. You look—"

"Like you lost the battle with the Granddaddy of all earthworms." Tess gave her a wink so Irmajean would know she was only kidding.

Irmajean decided on telling the truth, alert as circumstances would allow for the various responses. "I look exactly as you would expect me to look considering somebody hit me on the back of the head, dragged me into the hedge maze and left me to my own devices. My head hurts like—pardon me—like hell and, on top of that, I've lost my hat." She felt around on the top of her head as if to confirm that fact.

Rose Campion snickered and leaned over to give her a hug, overwhelming both Irmajean and Barron with the scent of patchouli. Irmajean didn't mind, but she could feel the lawyer recoil and could imagine him dropping his suit off at the cleaners tomorrow.

"Oh, Irmajean," Rose burbled, "I'm so glad you're all right. What would you have done if we hadn't been here?"

Ted appeared then to hand her the requested cup of tea. She smiled her thanks and wondered if she imagined the look of genuine concern she thought she saw in his eyes. "Thank you, Ted."

Tess pulled up a chair. "I don't know about anyone else, but I want to hear all the gory details of what happened and how you got inside the walls of Rosewood. You incredible woman, you."

Soon everyone was sitting there, attention focused on Irmajean who thought a cup of plain old black tea had never tasted so good. The only board member she couldn't see was Frederick Blumer, but that was because he was holding up the wall behind her. "I got here early this morning with every intention of looking for the hedge maze no one wanted to admit they knew about." Here she looked directly at Barron Lancaster who had the grace to look away. "But that newspaper clippings said existed. A bit of recent information had given me the hope I might find the entrance at the end of the rose garden." She took another restorative gulp of tea.

"I came armed with heavy duty clippers but even they couldn't make much of a dent in the blackberry bushes. While I worked, someone, I have no idea who," she was careful to make that point lest the villain try once again to rearrange her little gray cells, "crept up behind me and hit me on the back of the head. Then as I drifted in and out of consciousness he—she—it—whoever, dragged me into the maze and left me." She gingerly touched the back of her head. "I think I may have a slight concussion because it took awhile for the dizziness and nausea to pass enough so I could get up and moving. Every so often, Catkin would appear and give me moral support."

"Tell us," Rose asked, "is the maze passable or completely overgrown."

"Honestly, Rose, do you think she'd be here if it were impassable." Tess's expression told them what she thought of Rose's question.

Irmajean patted the deep pocket of her dress. "I had a pair of hand clippers with me so I was able to get through. Some places are more overgrown than others, but surprisingly, a trace of the original paths are evident if you look for them." She took another soothing swallow of tea.

"But how did you end up inside the house?" Millicent appreciated the fact that Irmajean hadn't mentioned confirmation of the maze came from her. Even though the major players were all dead and gone now, she'd always been a bit afraid of revealing her knowledge and connection with Rosewood in the days following Clarice Carmichael's marriage. There had been something secretive going on then, and it had filled her with fear. A fear she'd never been able to completely define, but that still existed in regards to the property. And yet, she couldn't stay away. Hadn't been able to say no when asked to serve on the board of directors. Once upon a time an invitation to Rosewood had been a coveted prize. And now as a member of the board, she could come and go whenever she wanted.

Irmajean obligingly continued her tale. "I had no idea whether I was walking towards the entrance or the very center of the maze. As it turned out, I was walking towards the center. There's a gazebo, benches, a statue of Atlas holding up the world." Her eyes lit up with remembrance. "What an addition this will make to our garden tours."

Tess nudged the story along. "Irmajean, if you don't hurry and tell us how you got inside this house from the far reaches of the garden, I'm going to be forced to shake it out of you."

It was all the reassurance Irmajean needed that Tess was thrilled she was all right. "Sorry, I got sidetracked. Now that I'm back where I should be, I can see the possibilities of my morning's discoveries. Anyway, to make a long story short, I was weary and not feeling too great so I sat down in the gazebo to rest. From that vantage point, I was able to see what looked like some kind of opening beneath the statue of Atlas. I decided to investigate, and while I was doing that I leaned against the statue, which moved, revealing steps and a tunnel."

Rose shuddered. "You entered a dark old tunnel not knowing what was in there?"

"There were lights most of the way. I found the cord by accident while reaching for Catkin who entered the tunnel as an advance guard. Once I knew I could see, I decided to investigate. I knew I could always come back to the maze if I had to. It seemed logical to assume the passage led to the house."

Irmajean hadn't missed the fact that the men present had been quiet throughout her entire narrative. Had they no questions or were they afraid they'd say too much if they said anything?

Hearing a noise behind her, she turned to see Frederick Blumer return to the hallway and in a business like manner begin to replace the section of paneling he'd removed in order to rescue her. He certainly wasn't wasting any time in restoring the appearance of the entryway to normal.

Tess crossed one shapely leg over the other. "Irmajean, do you think you could find your way through the maze now?"

"I don't know, but you can sure bet I'm going to try."

Millicent screwed up her courage to ask, "Was there anything in the tunnel?" Irmajean wondered how many people present would know she was lying if she said no? Perhaps with a murderer on the loose it was just as well to be open about what she'd discovered. "The passage is straight enough, but there's a circular room with a tile floor, a lectern, seats and a few other odds and ends. Obviously a meeting place at some time."

"You're kidding." This from Tess. "Do you know what that suggests?"

Irmajean finished her tea and suddenly wished she were at home. Her head felt as if she'd been clubbed, which she had, and now that she was safe she wanted nothing more than to go home and feel even safer. She knew the underground room suggested something, but she couldn't put her finger on just what, and it made her head hurt even more to speculate.

Millicent noticed that Irmajean was wilting before their eyes. "I think we should stop badgering Irmajean and see to it that she gets home safely. Irmajean, do you think you need to see a doctor?"

Irmajean shook her head. "All I need is a little rest." Someone had called the police and Frank Mallory arrived shortly. He took one look at his friend and decided his questions could wait. He took her home, but despite her protests, by way of the doctor's office, where it was confirmed she had a slight concussion. Otherwise, she was okay. With that diagnosis in hand, she finally got to go home. Glenn, horrified at the misadventures of his wife, helped her upstairs to bed.

"There's coffee in the pot, Frank. Help yourself. I'll get Irmajean settled, and then I'd like a word with you."

Frank, glad of an excuse for an on-duty break, did as asked. He even helped himself from a plate of cookies without invitation. Glenn would naturally have some questions. Unfortunately, he didn't think he was going to have any answers. About ten minutes later, Irmajean's husband came to the kitchen table and sat down heavily across from Chief Mallory. This was an older looking man from the one who had answered the door less than half and hour ago. The sight of his injured and disheveled wife had been a shock.

"Okay, Frank, can you tell me who you think tried to murder my wife?"

Eighteen

Glenn's bluntness took Frank aback. For a second he could think of nothing to say and when he did, he knew the words were useless as soon as they were out of his mouth. "We don't know that anyone tried to kill her."

Glenn slammed his fist against the table in a show of uncharacteristic anger, sloshing coffee over the top of Frank's cup. "Well you sure as heck could have fooled me. What is it somebody thinks she knows?"

Frank shook his head. "Maybe she can tell us when she gets to feeling better. I didn't want to badger her with too many questions."

"Well, you've more scruples than me. I mean to get to the bottom of this." Honey stroked his beard. "You're no more to blame than I am. I should have accompanied her to Rosewood or persuaded her to stay at home. I do think after today's episode she might be a little more careful."

Irmajean could hear the muffled sound of voices and suspected that Glenn and the Chief of Police were discussing her. And she imagined that their conversation was running along the same lines as her own thoughts. She would have to be more careful; to watch her back as they often suggested in crime novels. She knew something, but what? At the moment, her thoughts seemed somewhat jumbled, as if the categories had gotten mixed. The doctor had warned her that might be the case for a few days, but not to worry, it would go away. Meanwhile, she should rest. But how in the world was she going to rest an overactive imagination?

Irmajean was taken aback when Glenn announced. "Karl Webster is downstairs and wonders if you feel like a visitor?"

"Karl Webster?"

"Yes—"

"How strange." She'd never done more than exchange a very few words with him. "I wonder what he wants."

"Well, do you want to find out or not?"

"By all means, send him up."

"Do you want me to hang about, just in case?"

Honey was sweet, really, but she didn't think Karl of the brilliant orange dreadlocks was any danger to her. She was definitely curious as to why he was visiting her, however. "I don't think we need worry about him."

Karl sauntered into her bedroom, which was cozily stuffed with wicker furniture and needlepoint pillows depicting cats of various kinds. He spent a moment looking around and then handed her a lavish bouquet of sweet peas.

"Oh, Karl, thank you. They're beautiful!" And she buried her face in their sweet fragrance before plunking them stem first in a glass of water on the night stand.

"They're the first of my crop. Growing up in the city, I always wanted a garden, but until I settled in on Teddy's back forty there was never the opportunity."

"Well, you definitely have a green thumb. How about volunteering at Rosewood?"

"I just might do that. Care if I sit down?"

"No, sit anywhere you like."

Karl looked dubiously at a somewhat fragile appearing wicker chair before sitting carefully on it. "How are you feeling?"

"Not bad, considering. A bit woolly-headed, which the doctor gives me to understand is to be expected. But while my thoughts might tumble over one another, they're still active."

"Good, because I want to know everything that happened to you today."

"Why?" The visit was unexpected and the flowers sweet, Irmajean appreciated both, but she wasn't about to accept either at face value. While Karl's question didn't surprise her as much as his appearance in her bedroom, she didn't intend to answer it without knowing the reason behind it.

"Because I think it's time we get to the bottom of what's goin' on at Rosewood." He looked down, his gaze tracing a pattern on the rug, and his voice was a little shaky when he continued on. "I don't know if you knew it or not, but Priscilla and I were pretty good buds."

Irmajean jumped on his statement. "This is the first I've heard that. How come didn't I ever see you around Rosewood then?"

Karl had the grace to look a little sheepish. "I knew Teddy wouldn't approve. And I didn't want to get the old guy upset. So we had an agreement not to say anything to much of anybody. There was nothing serious between us—just friendship. We both like—liked—books, the opera and old houses. She had her degree in historic preservation, and I had mine in architecture although I've never sat for my license. For now, it's enough to not only know how things should be done, but why they're done the way they are. I'd stop by some mornings early just to visit, always bearing coffee and scones from the *Coffee Bean*. Sometimes Freddie would join us. You know how close-mouthed he is. Once warned, he wasn't about to tell anybody I'd been there. Now there's a guy with a serious thing for Rosewood. Pris would tease him, saying she was gonna knock a few walls out and see if she could find all those architectural things that were rumored to have once existed at Rosewood. Of course she was only kidding. No one respected the architectural integrity of the place more than she did. But it would get old Freddie goin'." He hesitated for a minute, and it was plain to see he was remembering.

"Why do you think it was that Frederick got so upset?"

"I suppose because he felt Rosewood to be complete the way it was."

"Except we're discovering the original house has been overlooked. To turn back the clock on Rosewood is to reveal the original. Even Frederick must see that."

"You would think so." He hesitated, scratching his scraggly beard. "Look, the reason I'm here is to do a little brainstorming. To see what you remember about today.

Because what happened to you has got to have some connection with Priscilla's murder. I believe in coincidence only to a point. I'm also prepared to share with you something I found, on the off chance it might have somethin' to do with what's goin' on around here. And I'll even tell you what I know first so you'll believe I'm on the level and not the guy who hit you over the head simply tryin' to find out what you remember. So, do we have a deal?"

Curious in spite of her headache, Irmajean nodded. "

"Teddy has more or less given me the run of his place, so long as I don't abuse his hospitality. Which I don't— usually. I keep a few brews in his fridge, and I borrow his downstairs shower, but that's it. He always made a point of the fact that I could have my run of the downstairs, but the upstairs was off limits. I never questioned this until Priscilla was murdered. Now Teddy jumps had every sound and had drank more sherry in the last couple days than he has in the last ten years. You were standin' right there with me when he and Lancaster were talkin. Somethin's got them both jumpy as hell. I decided I had to do something to get to the bottom of what's goin on."

"Go on."

"So I waited until I knew Teddy was gone for a while, and I took the opportunity to look around the off limits portion of the house. You wouldn't believe the things I found." Karl hesitated and shook his head as if he still couldn't believe it himself.

Irmajean straightened her nest of cushions and prodded. "Well? Don't stop now. What did you find?"

"A worn old carpet bag containing some really old clothes that looked like they might once have belonged to somebody from Asia. And there were some papers written in Chinese, Japanese, one of those languages. I can't tell the difference. There was even a little sack of coins—U.S.—and a small framed picture of a pretty young Asian woman. They weren't souvenirs, I can tell you that much."

"Is that all?" Irmajean was almost bursting with interest.

He scratched the matted back of his hair. "I don't know if you're gonna believe me. I'm not sure I believe it. Geez, I might have expected to find a lot of things in Teddy's attic, but never a mummy."

Irmajean knew her jaw dropped and that her mouth hung open unattractively. To say she was stunned was an understatement. "Are you sure?"

He nodded, "Oh, yeah."

"An Egyptian mummy?"

He laughed heartily at that thought. "Hell, no! I'd say from the clothes and the other stuff I found that it's the guy who owned the carpet bag."

"Oh, you've got to be mistaken." She saw him shake his head. "Karl, no one, least of all Ted, would keep a dead man in his attic. Think of—well, you know. The ramifications. Ted doesn't even like to go into the garden because of the bugs and slugs. He'd be the last person in the world, and I do mean the last, to have a body in the attic"

"I'm not kidding you. There's a dead man in Teddy's attic. And what's more, Teddy knows it." He ducked his head and then gave her a sheepish grin. "He caught me snoopin'."

Irmajean shook her head. "What did he say? I'm assuming you asked him who it was."

"That he was Rosewood's shame."

"Oh, dear."

Webster eyed her suspiciously. "You sound as if you might have an idea who it is—was."

Certain things were beginning to fall into place for Irmajean or at least seemed to. But would these fragments come together to make a whole? "Ted and Barron are both very protective of Rosewood. They don't want it to fall into private hands. I always assumed that was because Chalmers had been their friend. Maybe that was only part of it. Maybe they didn't want the property out of their control because they were afraid of what someone might find."

Evidently Karl's thoughts had been continuing along the same lines. "But that doesn't tell me who I found in Teddy's attic."

"I think I can tell you that. I'd say it's likely you found a servant of Clarice's who went missing about the same time her husband did."

Karl scratched away at his flaming dreadlocks. "But what's he doin' in Teddy's attic?"

"That is an excellent question, and I'll bet the key to a lot of what's going on, especially when coupled with Ted's comment he was Rosewood's shame. Wasn't Ted at all concerned you might tell someone what you'd found?"

"My keepin' quiet was pretty much assumed."

"And yet you told me."

"I thought I could keep quiet, but it nagged at me until I knew I had to tell someone. After the attack on you, I decided you were the one to tell."

"Karl, you're very loyal to Ted, aren't you?"

"He's not a bad old guy. A little fussy, a little set in his ways. But harmless."

"Yet he's been keeping a body in his attic all these years."

"If I'm doin' my math right, Teddy wouldn't a been much more than a teenager at the time."

"As we've unfortunately learned from our nightly news dose of mayhem, no one is apparently ever too young to commit an atrocity. Let's hope, however, that Ted, and probably Barron, have simply been hiding evidence of someone else's wrong doing. Don't ever underestimate the importance of family to either man. Barron's air of superiority is genuine. He really does believe his family's pioneer status gives him precedence over newcomers. And I think he's capable of most anything that would preserve what he sees as the sanctity of his family name. And Millicent claims that the fathers of both men were heavily involved with Willowby."

"Yeah, Teddy hangs on to that mausoleum of a house because it's been in the family who knows how long. He hasn't changed a thing since his mother died. There's the most godawful wallpaper on the walls and the plumbing sounds like it's alive or at the very least something is living in the pipes. You flush the toilet on the main floor and it sounds like somebody running up and down the stairs. I about went straight up the first time I heard it, 'cause I thought at the time I was alone in the house.

When I asked Teddy once why he didn't redecorate, he said, 'Mother wouldn't like it.'" He shook his head in disbelief. "Geez, the old broad's been dead forever, why should she care if he redecorated? Or even opened the curtains for that matter." He shuddered. "Five minutes in that place and you're lookin' over your shoulder for ghosts."

"Karl, will you show me this body?"

He seemed somewhat taken aback at her request. "You don't mean right now?"

"I do, but I don't. I suppose I've had all the excitement I need for one day, all things considered. Besides, Honey would never let me out of the house. But I do want to see it and soon."

"Teddy won't like it."

"Does Ted have to know?"

"If I'm gonna start runnin' guided tours through his house, he's sure as hell gonna find out."

"Listen, Karl. A man disappeared over fifty years ago from Rosewood and very possibly was murdered. Just days ago Priscilla Norris made a discovery. Then she was murdered. It's been obvious all along that Ted was afraid of something. Perhaps even hiding something. I think you discovered at least a part of what that was. Perhaps Ted knows nothing about what happened to Priscilla. Perhaps his fears that the past is somehow connected with her murder are groundless. Perhaps not. But we can't overlook the possibility. I won't tell Frank Mallory. I won't tell anyone unless I think there's a link between the body in Ted's attic and Priscilla's murder. While I'm not quite as fond of Ted as you obviously are, I don't want to cause any trouble for anyone unless it's necessary."

Karl had to admit that the probability of a missing man being the mummy in Ted's attic wasn't looking too good for the old guy. "I don't think Teddy could have killed Priscilla."

"I'm inclined to agree with you." Although she had to admit things weren't looking too good for Ted either. "But he might know something that would tell us who did." She all but held her breath, while realizing she couldn't force Karl to show her the body. Nevertheless, she said, "You have to show me the body."

"Then what?"

"What do you mean, then what?"

"Just what it sounds like I mean. After I show you the body, what are we gonna do?"

"Maybe we won't have to do anything."

Karl thought about fussy old Teddy, pottering about his barn of a house while making certain everything occupied the same space it had occupied practically forever. "Maybe we could sneak him out, give him a proper burial and not tell a soul."

"Karl, murder is murder."

Nineteen

Glenn walked in to find his wife in a pensive mood. "So, are you going to tell me what Karl had to tell you?"

Irmajean turned onto her side, propped herself up on her elbow and rested her head on her hand. "You know, I'm a bit suspicious of Mr. Webster."

"You surely don't think he's guilty in Priscilla's murder?" There was genuine surprise in his voice.

"No, not at all. But I don't think he's quite who he seems. He likes to give the impression he's nothing more than a pot smoking, good old boy, but every so often that bit of cover slips. Karl is very well-educated and he's genuinely concerned about Ted. Why?"

"How should I know?"

"I meant that why rhetorically. Nevertheless, I would like to know what Karl sees in Ted Meyers that the rest of us have missed. He worries about Ted, and he doesn't like the way Barron Lancaster treats him at all. Why?"

"If you want to know the answer to that, you'll have to ask Karl."

Irmajean, her arm tingling, turned over on to her back. "I wonder if in the end everything will turn out to be connected."

"I suppose that depends on what you mean by connected and by everything."

"Rosewood, Karl, Ted, Priscilla's murder, the mummy..."

"Mummy? What are you talking about?"

She felt a certain smugness at having regained his attention so effectively. "Karl found a mummy in the attic of Ted's house."

"You're kidding me?" Irmajean wished she could preserve the expression on her husband's face.

"Well, I haven't seen it myself, but Karl swears there is one. He also found a carpetbag and other things—pictures, coins that make me suspect he's located Clarice Carmichael's long missing servant. The one we saw in the photograph album."

"You're sure about this? Could Karl be making this up? I'd believe almost anything before I'd believe Ted's been storing a corpse in his attic for who knows how long. What's Karl been smoking? And what's he doing snooping around in Ted's attic?"

"He was concerned over Ted and felt there was something he was hiding. So the first opportunity he got, he explored the parts of the house Ted proclaimed off limits. He didn't bargain on finding what he did."

"I should think not." Then the suspicion suddenly dawned on him of the purpose behind Karl's visit. "He wants to show you this body, doesn't he?"

Irmajean, pleased, nodded. "He's agreed to show it to me, I'm not sure if he exactly *wants* to or not."

"Why you?"

"I suppose because somebody hit me over the head."

Glenn rubbed his face and groaned. This was a line of logic he was suddenly too tired to pursue.

~ * ~

Two days passed after Karl's visit. Two days of starting and then abandoning one paperback mystery after another. Irmajean was restless, bored, and badly wanting to return to Rosewood. Inactivity, she thought, was highly overrated. Was anybody tending the roses which would soon be in their prime? Was anybody feeding Catkin? Would she be able to find the entrance to the maze? Life at Rosewood was going on without her and that knowledge did nothing to cheer her. The doctor had wanted her to rest for a week, but since she was driving both of them crazy, he had said maybe tomorrow she could put in an hour or two of work. *An hour or two!* Who was scheduling new events and making certain old ones were moving along as they should with both her and Priscilla absent? Ted might be able to answer the phone and sort the mail, but she knew from experience that decision-making was not his strong suit. They'd all worked too hard to get Rosewood up and running and somebody was needed at the helm if it was going to continue.

Her head was no longer aching, although her thought processes were still a bit muddled. But that wouldn't keep her from pulling weeds or dead heading the roses or seeing if she could locate the entrance to the maze. Good heavens, there was a wedding scheduled in the rose garden in two weeks and every bit of time was needed to get ready for it. Would the other volunteer gardeners know what to do? She'd always taken charge, and they'd been happy to let her do so, but perhaps she'd better give them a reminder call.

The phone rang just as she reached to pick it up. Since their home phone was also their business phone, she always let Honey answer first, because nine and a half times out of ten the call was for him. However, when she heard Honey's footsteps on the stairs, she knew it was for her. "Hello?"

"Irmajean, it's Karl Webster. How are you feeling?"

"Better, bored...What can I do for you?"

"Teddy left a little while ago. Barron stopped by for him, and they're going into Portland. Do you think your husband will let you out, because now's a good time for me to show you what I found?" He sounded a little anxious, and she hoped he wasn't getting cold feet.

"Only if I bring him along."

"The more the merrier. I'll be waiting."

Irmajean called down from the top of the stairs. "Glenn, we're going for a drive."

"And who is this *we* business?"

"You and me if you can spare the time. If not I'm sure I'll be fine driving out to Ted's."

He gave her his you've-got-to-be-kidding look. "Good grief, woman. Someone tried to kill you just days ago. You can't go gallivanting all over the countryside."

"And I can't sit around here growing moss either. I'll be fine. I am fine. Besides, you can bet I won't turn my back on anyone. That was Karl Webster. Ted and Barron have just left for Portland. So this is the perfect time for him to show me—us—what he found in Ted's attic."

"The idea of breaking and entering doesn't bother you?"

"We won't be breaking and entering. Karl has a key."

"Which he was given for his use. Not to give guided tours."

"Honey, listen. Frank Mallory is getting nowhere trying to solve Priscilla Norris's murder. Perhaps, just perhaps, Karl has stumbled upon something that might help. We can't afford to let this opportunity pass."

"Irmajean, just say Karl really has found a dead body in Ted's attic. From his description, it must have been there a long time. So how could it have anything to do with Priscilla's murder?"

"Because *everything* connected with Rosewood has something to do with the past. If Millicent can be believed, there were strange goings on and secrets swept under the rug."

"Which is where we should leave them. Besides, Millicent Morgan is a writer, and you know how they embroider on the truth."

"If nothing had happened to Priscilla then I would agree with you."

Glenn shook his head. "I don't see the connection with Ted's attic."

"At the moment it's not exactly clear to me either, but I'm sure it soon will be."

"Irmajean, that's not a good enough reason."

"Look, Millicent mentioned that Clarice's Chinese servant disappeared about the time she divorced her husband. That Clarice hinted at evil doings on the part of said husband. At the same time, Clarice ceased hosting any social activities at Rosewood. The rest of the help was let go and the garden neglected. Logically, all these things must be connected. And perhaps that connection lays waiting in Ted's attic."

"Then we should tell Frank."

"No! No, that would only get Karl in trouble, not to mention Ted."

"And you think once we see what Karl wants to show us that neither of those eventualities is likely to happen? Irmajean, if Karl has really found a body then I'm going to tell the police. To do anything else would be senseless."

She patted his arm. "Let's see what Karl's found first. Now let's hurry, or Ted will return before we get there."

Karl was sitting on the front steps when they drove up to Ted's house. He stood up and sauntered over to them. "I thought you were never gonna get here."

Irmajean glanced over at her husband. "There were those of us who took some persuading."

Glenn turned to Karl. "If you've really discovered what you say, then we're going to have to tell the police."

Karl raised a hand in protest. "I don't want to make any trouble for old Teddy."

"If old Teddy has a body in the attic, then he's already made his own trouble."

Irmajean and Karl exchanged looks, and she simply shook her head. "Why don't you show us, Karl. We can talk about what we're going to do afterwards." She knew that Glenn was right, and she suspected that Karl did too. Otherwise, he would never have turned and entered the house.

The past settled over them as they stood in the entry hall of Ted Myers' home. The smell of dusty old things dominated, and Irmajean looked around in awe at the faded maroon wallpaper and heavy dark furniture. Curtains were drawn over most of the windows, although a little light did seep through a crack or two. "It's so dark in here."

"Teddy's afraid any sunlight will fade the furniture. I opened a curtain once, and I thought he'd have apoplexy. His response is always the same. *Mother wouldn't like it if she was here.*"

Irmajean had often wondered what the inside of Ted's house must look like. Various comments he made had her suspecting a museum, but this had more the feel of a mausoleum. She was trailing along, taking the time to look in the various rooms. Glenn turned to her. "Come on, Irmajean, let's keep moving."

"But we have lots of time. Karl said they were going to Portland."

"That doesn't mean we could or should prowl the length and breadth of Ted's house."

She hurried to catch up with the two men, for the moment squelching her curiosity, albeit reluctantly. They climbed the stairs to the second floor, and she barely resisted stopping to look at the various portraits. She loved old pictures and the stories they told. Hadn't she learned as much from the photograph album found at Rosewood as she had from anything? She whispered to Honey. "You know, it has always seemed strange to me that as family proud as Ted is, he never entertains, never has anyone to the house."

"Maybe he's afraid someone will go poking in his attic."

"Then why has he given Karl the run of the place?"

"Good question."

Heavy velvet draperies covered the windows on the second floor and a Burgundy toned wallpaper dominated. Karl flipped a light switch so they could at least see where they were going. "Teddy doesn't use anything but the first floor now. He probably hasn't even been up here in years."

Irmajean couldn't imagine having a house and only living in part of it. She'd rather have two rooms she lived in than a whole house she didn't. But then, she hadn't inherited a piece of history, either. Again she trailed along behind the two men, opening a door here, peering at a picture there. Light from the hallway barely penetrated the gloom of the bedrooms, but it did to the point she could see a bureau whose top was cluttered with picture frames. Glancing at the others and seeing that they weren't paying any attention to her, she slipped into the room and switched on the light.

She knew she only had a few minutes, and so she didn't waste any time looking around the bedroom, but made straight for the chest of drawers. Picking up first one picture and then another. They weren't terribly interesting, except for one. It was a lovely, hand-tinted wedding portrait of two people. Irmajean, half expecting it and yet still surprised, recognized Ted—young, surprisingly handsome, beaming with happiness. Beside him was the young woman she'd seen in the photograph album from Rosewood. This was, she suspected, the Siren from the East. A frothy white veil adorned her luxurious hair. Hair as brilliantly orange as Karl Webster's.

She heard a noise in the doorway and turned to find Karl watching her.

"So now you know."

"Ted is your father?" All she sought was confirmation.

Karl nodded, while leaning against the doorjamb.

"What happened? Why didn't—doesn't anybody know?"

"A few people did. Teddy, Barron—After Mom returned home, she kept in touch with Teddy. They wrote letters, exchanged gifts, and when he went back East to visit her, they were married. They had six glorious months together—those were always Mom's words—before his mother put her oar in the water." Here Karl affected a high-pitched voice. "Ted needed to come home, she wasn't feeling well; the family affairs needed his guiding hand. Etc., etc., etc.," He glanced down at the rug, to where he'd been worrying a small hole with the toe of his boot.

"What happened then?"

"Mom was pregnant and not feeling too well, so she didn't make the trip with Teddy. I think she thought he'd sort his mother out and be back. After all, he was no kid. But first one thing and then another kept coming up, and it became increasingly obvious that Teddy's mother controlled not only Teddy but the family money. He never did return to my mother. Never saw anything more than pictures of me until I turned up on his doorstep about a year ago."

Irmajean didn't miss the sadness in Karl's voice.

"I admit I came out here at first to get even with the man who broke my mother's heart. She never gave up hope he'd return to her. There was something about Teddy she loved, could never let go of. And my mother was a sought after beauty. What she saw in him remains a mystery. They never divorced, and she died still hoping he'd return to her. He did support us financially. Paid for my very high-priced education, but he was definitely not there for her or for me."

"Why do you suppose he didn't bring you out here once his mother was gone? Or wouldn't your mother have come?"

"Many times Mom asked if she couldn't move out, but he always had some excuse. After a while, her pride kept her from asking again. But I'm beginning to wonder if the reason Teddy stayed here, bound to this house and this stagnant way of life had to do with what's in the attic. Come on, let's get a move on."

Irmajean followed Karl from the bedroom. They came to a stop beneath a cord that dangled from the ceiling. He gave it a tug and a staircase descended. "I'll go first and turn on the lights. Glenn, why don't you let Irmajean follow me."

If the first two floors of the house were dusty, Irmajean didn't know what word would describe the attic. The air was fusty, close and a thick layer of dust and cobwebs covered everything.

"You can see why I don't think anyone has been up here in some time."

She could indeed. Dust just didn't cover things, it lay like a furry gray shroud over everything in the narrow room that she saw at a glance ran the length of Ted's house. Irmajean felt Glenn crowd in behind her, and she moved away from the stair entrance. "Phew! This place could stand a little maid service." But he spoke in a whisper. She noticed that they all did.

"It's—he's over here under the window."

They followed Karl toward the light filtering in through the small oval window at one end of the long room. There on a cot, neatly tucked in as if ready for sleep, was an unsettling mixture of bones and taut skin. It wasn't very pretty but then neither was it frightening. Whatever had happened to this person had obviously happened a long time ago.

Irmajean glanced over at Honey and up at Karl who had to stoop to accommodate his height to the slope of the roof. "Did he ask you not to tell anyone?"

Karl shook his head. "The more I got to thinkin' about it, the more I wondered if maybe Teddy wanted me to tell. Wanted it all to be over with." He stood silent for a moment. "What do you think?"

The closeness of the attic and the lack of air were starting to bother Irmajean. Her head was buzzing and much as she hated to admit it, she was feeling a bit light headed. "I think I'd like to go downstairs." And she beat a hasty retreat. Not until they were outside in the bracing fresh air did she say another word. "Karl, I appreciate what you've shown us. You took a chance on harming Ted, and I know that's the last thing you want to do."

"So what do you think I should do now? What are you going to do?"

"I don't think you should do anything. Just go about your life as usual. I've really done about all that I can today, but Glenn," and she glanced over at her husband with a smile, "and I will visit Rosewood tomorrow. And maybe, just maybe we can get to the bottom of this."

Glenn said nothing more until they were in the car and headed toward home. Then he glanced over at Irmajean who rested, eyes closed with her head against the door. "Are you okay?"

"I'm tired, but I think I really do see a light at the end of the tunnel so to speak. And I mean that both literally and figuratively. I think the answer to what has happened is in the maze and the tunnel beneath it. And I think it's all linked with that body in Ted's attic. There was a book resting on the lectern in that tunnel room, Honey. I should have taken it when I was down there. The best I can do now is hope somebody hasn't removed it. Because I'd be willing to bet the answer lies within its pages."

"You're not going back in there!" It was more an admonishment than a command.

"I have to, but I want you to go with me. I'm not about to venture in there by myself, no."

"If Frederick has repaired the entrance to the tunnel on the house side, do you think we can reopen it without causing any damage?"

"We'll go in through the maze."

"Do you really think we can do that?"

Irmajean nodded emphatically. "When we get home you make us a nice cup of tea and I'll get out my magazine that has pictures of the Hampton Court maze. They're supposed to be identical according to the newspaper clippings. We also know from Millicent that the entrance to the maze was at the end of the rose garden. That will be our starting point. I'll draw us a detailed map, and we'll come armed with shears and hedge clippers."

Her long suffering husband groaned, "And maybe a trail of breadcrumbs."

"Seriously, that might not be a bad idea. Meanwhile, do you think I could get you to stop at the store for some aspirin?"

"Headache?"

"Definitely."

They drove along in silence for the next few minutes until Glenn turned the car into the grocery store parking lot. "I'll run in and get it." He was already unfastening his seat belt.

"Would you mind? I'm really not feeling too great." A cup of tea and a rest were sounding better and better all the time. She leaned her head against the window of the car door and closed her eyes while waiting for her husband to return. When the driver's side door opened she straightened up.

He handed her a small sack. "Sorry I was so long, but I ran into Frederick Blumer and he wanted to talk a minute."

"Frederick wanted to talk?"

"I was looking for the aspirin and saw him perusing the hair dye section. He felt compelled to explain that he sometimes used it to mix his own woodworking stain."

"I've never heard of such a thing."

"Neither have I but then how much woodworking have you and I done?"

"Granted, next to none, but it still strikes me as strange." But then she recalled it wasn't the first unusual explanation she'd heard from Frederick. There was also the day he'd elaborated on the prospect of an underground tunnel at Rosewood.

Twenty

The next day Irmajean was feeling good enough to at long last attempt finding the garden maze. She'd expected her husband to argue with her and viewed him with suspicion when he didn't.

His response was simply, "I've learned to deal with the inevitable."

Irmajean was feeling positively perky when they arrived at Rosewood and relieved that there were no other cars around. Eager as she was to get busy, she couldn't help stopping here and there to smell a flower or admire a plant's progress. Bulbs were blooming everywhere. She'd only been away a couple of days, but it was the season for constant change. "You know, Honey, much as I dislike Barron and as crazy as Ted drives me—I really don't want them to have killed Priscilla."

When they reached the end of the Rose garden, Irmajean produced a carefully hand drawn sketch from the voluminous pocket of her rose sprigged garden smock. It was a rather primitive reproduction of the Hampton Court

Maze. She studied it for a moment, walked over to a tangle of blackberry vines and pointed to the spot where she'd been hit on the head. "Clip here."

Two hours later, they stood before the gazebo in the heart of the maze. Glenn turned an admiring gaze on his disheveled-looking wife. They were both sweaty, dirty and covered with twigs and leaves, but they had reached their goal in what he considered record time. He had doubted the probable effectiveness of her drawing, but she had proved his doubts to be groundless. *And* she had found her hat. "You really did your homework yesterday."

Irmajean was not above basking in a bit of glory. She turned a beaming smile on Honey. "It helped that I had passed this way once before. Therefore, I knew that while it was overgrown, it wasn't impassable. And the newspaper articles Pricilla had found emphasized that it was a replica of the renowned Hampton Court Maze. Now," and she drew in a deep, deep breath. "Let's have a close look at this gazebo."

Glenn collapsed on the stone bench thoughtfully provided for the weary wanderer. "What do you say we have a look at it from a sitting down position?"

Irmajean plunked down on the opposite end of the bench. Despite the energy expended, she was feeling much better than the afternoon before. "Sounds good to me. I see the entrance to the tunnel is still open. Which I hope means no one has been here since my escapade."

"Unless someone has deliberately left it that way to make us think no one has been here. We need to consider that possibility—and to watch our backs." He gave her a steely look.

She'd gotten up that morning feeling rested and more her old self. With a clearer head than on her previous visit to the gazebo, she looked around.

"What are you looking at?" Glenn glanced quickly around as if he might surprise something or someone creeping up on him.

"That stained glass window above your head. It's a memorial. It didn't register with me the other day, but then I guess that isn't surprising." She walked over to it, reaching a finger up to trace the outline of a man's face— dark eyes, full beard and the single word across the bottom of the picture—*Walter.*

She turned toward Honey with a look of absolute frustration. "I'd forgotten. Perhaps it's more correct to say I hadn't forgotten so much as I hadn't realized the importance of something."

"And what's that?"

"That Clarice Carmichael had a brother."

"But I thought he left town under a cloud?"

"But that doesn't mean Clarice wouldn't have still loved him and remembered him."

Honey gestured at the picture. "Wouldn't this memorial indicate he was dead?'

"Maybe, maybe not. Perhaps it was simply a place for remembering a better time. Perhaps this memorial was created by and known only to Clarice. A place she didn't have to explain to anyone because no one knew about it.

She'd ridded herself of her husband and closed Rosewood to everyone."

She shook her head in disbelief but said nothing. The identity of Priscilla's killer and her own attacker now seemed glaringly obvious, and it filled her with overwhelming sadness. She hoped against hope that she was wrong, but suspected and feared that she wasn't. Why hadn't she guessed? Why hadn't any of them guessed at the connection?

"Does this sudden revelation have anything to do with what happened to Priscilla and you?"

"I'm afraid so. Still, maybe I'm wrong. I have been before. Come, let's hit the tunnel. You did remember a flashlight, didn't you?"

"One for each of us." And he handed her a small, yet powerful, pocket flash.

Irmajean started down the steps. "I'll go first and find the light cord." She was as good as her word, and soon they were traveling the dimly lit corridor that connected the maze with Rosewood.

Glenn stayed close behind her until they reached the small circular room where Irmajean bustled over to the podium. With an almost desperate grab, she reached for the book lying there. "You don't know how afraid I was this would be missing." While Glenn walked over to open the cupboard, she quickly tried to scan its pages. The writing was nearly illegible and the lighting poor, nevertheless because of their familiarity a name or two jumped from the pages.

"Have a look at this." Turning, she saw he held up a full-length robe covered with arcane symbols. "It looks as if some self-styled secret society used to meet here."

"Why do you say self-styled?"

"Because I don't recognize the meeting location, the robes or the symbols as belonging to any lodge or organization I'm familiar with—or ever heard of for that matter."

"I think you're right." And she held up the book she'd been so relieved to find, having feared her assailant might have thought to remove it. "This contains a list of names—some of them quite familiar—and the title of their office. Look at this," and she pointed a dirty finger at the top name. "Bertram Willowby, High Magician." She snapped the book shut. "Millicent said that he was a cruel, wicked man. That he taunted Clarice's Chinese servant. Something happened that caused Clarice to step back from society; to live the life of a recluse except for work; to willfully neglect her show place garden. I think that something is directly connected with the body in Ted's attic—and to whatever transpired in this room."

"So Ted probably didn't mean he was Rosewood's shame but that what happened to him was?"

Irmajean was about to answer, "More than likely," when a grating sound came from the entrance to the tunnel and the lights winked out. She instinctively reached out for Honey, but her hand met only thin air. "Where are you and what was that?"

"I'm over here and *that* was no doubt the sound of you and I being trapped. Just a minute." Within seconds a thin beam of light sliced the darkness, and Irmajean breathed just a little easier while fumbling for the flashlight buried in her pocket. "The darkness is rather total, isn't it?"

Glenn nodded, although he suspected she couldn't see it. "Well, we are underground."

Irmajean edged a little closer. "Do you think we're down here alone?"

She'd been listening for any sounds that might indicate otherwise.

"Oh, yeah. Whoever pushed Atlas back in place is counting on trapping us like a pair of moles."

Irmajean found the thought rather disconcerting. "Surely whoever must realize I know the way out. That I've passed this way before." Then she uttered a disquieting thought she couldn't keep to herself. "Frederick resealed the tunnel at the other end."

"Don't panic, we'll be okay. Let's retrace our steps, and see if we can figure out how Atlas is moved from this side."

But they couldn't, not even after Irmajean broke two already stubby fingernails trying. "It's no use, but at least we can turn the lights back on. We can be grateful whoever didn't disable them."

Glenn grunted. "Did you think at any time that somebody might have been following us?"

"I was more interested in getting from Point A to Point B."

"Then let's head in the direction of Point B." They moved along in silence for a few moments. "When you were in here the other day did you notice any other tunnels or rooms?"

"No, I don't think there are any. Unless—it was pretty dark at the other end, and I was frazzled from the blow on my head. Sorry I'm not any more help."

"Never mind. We'll get out of here. Don't worry."

Which is precisely what she was doing. This was Glenn's first time in the tunnel so he could be optimistic. She, on the other hand, remembered only too well the sense of panic that had descended on her when she'd reached what seemed a dead end. But she knew if there was a way out to be found, they would find it. Or so she kept telling herself as they trudged toward Rosewood.

Twenty-one

They switched off their flashlights to conserve power and navigated by the light from the string of bulbs along the ceiling. Illumination that was almost non-existent by the time they reached the end of the line. Irmajean remembered that all enveloping blackness gradually descending as she moved toward what she hoped was the house and a way out. It had been like walking into a black fog. Today was different. Today she wasn't alone. Irmajean's thoughts were so all consuming that she collided with Glenn when he stopped abruptly. "You might signal when you're going to stop."

"Take a look." And he beamed his light around the end of the tunnel. There was the blank wall, now so carefully replaced. Over to the side and easily missed without a light, was a metal ladder rising up into the darkness.

"Where do you suppose it leads?" Irmajean couldn't keep the excitement from her voice.

"There's only one way to find out. Shine your light upward while I climb."

Irmajean listened to her husband grunt and groan his way up what was an obviously narrow space. "Are you finding anything?" she called. When there wasn't an immediate answer she called out anxiously. "Honey, are you okay?"

She heard a scraping sound as if something were being moved against its will. When Honey replied his voice seemed to come from far away. "Well, well. What do you know?"

"What!"

"Can you manage that ladder?"

"I suppose." She wasn't very good with heights, but she thought the quarters snug enough that she wouldn't fall.

"I'll beam the light downward while trying not to blind you."

Irmajean pocketed her own flashlight and began inching her way up the ladder. In no time at all, Honey had hold of her wrists and was pulling her free of the narrow earthen tube. Only then did she realize that they were standing at the foot of the staircase leading to the tower. To one side lay the cover that must have accounted for the scraping sound she'd heard. There also was the door that had once led from the base of the tower and was now boarded up on the outside as if it had never existed. Had Clarice done that or the infamous Bertram when he instituted his secret society?

"For a minute, I was afraid I wouldn't be able to budge the cover or that somebody had nailed it in place. I'm not sure from this side that a person would have known it was there unless of course they knew about the tunnel. Especially with all the junk tossed down here." And he kicked at a broken board.

"That would explain why the police overlooked it when they removed Priscilla's body from the staircase." And she glanced upward. "They probably assumed that boarded up door was the only other entrance to the stairs."

Irmajean was more than happy to let him take the lead as they climbed the circular staircase hidden for so many years within the walls of the tower. Only when they stepped out into the attic did she realize that they had passed the spot where Priscilla's body had been found. They'd had to move cautiously because of broken steps and debris that had been thrown down the stairwell probably when it was boarded up. But eventually they were stooping through the opening torn in the tower wall. The fresh air of the well-ventilated attic was more than welcome.

Now Irmajean moved ahead, and Glenn took a hold of her arm. "Where are you going in such a hurry?"

"The library—there are several family photographs on the wall and I need to be sure."

"Sure of what?"

"Of who killed Priscilla. If I'm right... If I'm right, Priscilla was killed because of an obsession."

Glenn followed his slightly maddening wife at almost breakneck speed downstairs and into the library. There curled up in a slightly worn recliner was Catkin who looked up and yawned at their entrance, something just barely visible between his paws.

"What brought Frederick to Pirate's Cove? I wondered the same about Karl, but of course now that I know Ted is his father I can understand why he came and stayed. But quiet Frederick was always a mystery. He donated so much time to Rosewood. Lavished so much loving care on preserving the house and more than anyone resisted change. He was obsessed with restoring Rosewood to the way it was. Priscilla used to tease him about tearing out the walls in the entry hall and upstairs in the attic in search of the hidden places that were supposed to exist. I thought it was obvious that she was only teasing him, that he would realize that. How she persuaded him to remove part of the wall in the attic... Or maybe she wasn't teasing him. And maybe that's why he killed her."

"Irmajean, you're losing me."

She had moved over to a series of faded photographs framed and easy to overlook on a short wall behind Catkin's recliner. There he let his gaze move as he knew hers was doing from picture to picture. And there he saw what she was looking for. Confirmation of the truth that had dawned on her in the gazebo.

"It was Frederick who first put me on to the possibility of a tunnel beneath the property. I don't think he meant to tell me and when it slipped out, he sought to cover it up with some story about the tunnel being exposed when it snowed slightly last winter. Snow hadn't stuck because of the warmth within the tunnel. I thought about that more than once, not so much because of his explanation, but because I wondered if a tunnel or tunnels really did exist. We'd had a Board of Directors meeting scheduled the day of the snowfall but postponed it. Frederick explained when he was telling me about the tunnel that he'd driven out here anyway that day. And that was how he'd noticed the snow didn't stick some places. We held the meeting the next day but Frederick was absent. The explanation was that he was in Astoria with his dog who was having surgery to replace the ligaments in one of her back legs. He'd stayed up there all week in a motel so he could be near her. I only remembered that when I really looked at that memorial window in the gazebo. Frederick knew about the tunnel not because of the snow fall but from his father, Clarice Carmichael's long lost brother."

"I really wish you weren't quite so clever, Irmajean. I really do. I've always liked you, and I really don't want to have to hurt you. You either, Mr. Lloyd."

Both Irmajean and Glenn turned toward the doorway. It crossed Irmajean's mind that Frederick Blumer was a very big man. "Did you try to lock us in the tunnel, Frederick?"

"I did."

"Why didn't you try to escape then?"

He shrugged. "Where would I have gone? I've knocked about the country all my life, staying here longer than I've ever stayed anywhere. I never knew my mother and was thirteen when I lost my dad. He was way past being a young man by the time I was born. But I never forgot the stories of his home that he told me. I was always going to come here. Then one day, I found out I had two maybe three years at the most to live. So I headed west and found Rosewood. The old house needed me, and it became the family I didn't have."

"Why didn't your father ever return?"

"He couldn't. He'd stolen money from the bank where he worked here. People have long memories when it comes to money, and he was spared prosecution by leaving town."

"How old are you Frederick? Older than you seem?"

"Fifty—I dyed my beard and hair so I'd seem younger. You almost caught me that time in the grocery store, Mr. Lloyd. It took some quick thinking on my part."

Irmajean nodded. "You fooled us for a bit since neither one of us knows a thing about woodworking. Although I did wonder why on the rare times when you grow talkative it's always to impart some unusual bit of information. Why not just say hello to Honey, nod and walk on? Why feel like you owed him an explanation? And the tunnels. Why mention them at all, particularly when it placed you at the scene on a day memory reminded me you were in Astoria with your dog."

"I've always had the problem of saying too much or too little. And the tunnels fascinated me. Didn't you ever wonder why there were working lights down there after all these years? I'm the one who replaced them."

Before Irmajean had a chance to respond, Glenn stepped forward barely able to keep himself under control as he confronted the man who had attacked his wife. "Why did you hit Irmajean over the head? What made you think she was any threat to you?"

"She's a smart woman, but she asks too many questions. I knew it was only a matter of time before she put two and two together—just as she has done. I thought if I frightened her then maybe she'd back off, let the police handle things. I didn't think I had much to fear from them. Instead, attacking her seems to have made her more determined."

"Because it gave me time to think; to wonder what in the world I knew." She studied him for a moment. "Wouldn't you have been better off just to shave your beard? Then you wouldn't have been such a look alike to Clarice's brother and your father, Walter."

"Because without the beard I look exactly like my grandfather. I knew my father was the black sheep of the family. He never made any secret of that. So I figured there wouldn't be many pictures of him around—if any. I thought the best disguise was simply to look too young to have any connection with him."

"But why kill Priscilla?" It was a question she had to ask before the shadow she'd noticed moving in the hallway took shape and spoiled her chance to put what she considered a satisfactory finish to this investigation.

She saw Frederick stiffen and a frown crease his forehead. "I didn't really think she'd ever harm the house, even though she teased she might if the end satisfied the means. Then one day I was making some repairs to the second floor stairs, and I heard the sound of ripping wood coming from the attic. I found her kneeling by a hole she'd made in the wall, ecstatic over her discovery of the tower staircase. I guess I never realized how much she wanted to find Rosewood's secret places. The last thing she said to me was that she knew I could fix the damaged wall like new again."

His voice was so sad that Irmajean could have cried. "But you didn't fix it. You left it so she'd be found."

"I didn't think anyone would ever suspect me if I left the wall as it was. Priscilla would have been found eventually and if the wall had been as good as new, everyone would have known it was me. She should never have harmed my house. If anyone has a right to Rosewood and its history, then it's me."

If the poker he wielded hadn't actually done the job, the sheer unexpected appearance of Ted would have. Like someone with a demon on his tail, he ran screaming from the hallway, a fireplace poker raised above his head until he brought it crashing down on Frederick's shoulder. Irmajean could hear the crack of bone as Frederick fell to his knees.

"Ted!" Irmajean and Glenn cried out in unison.

Frederick writhed in agony as Ted hovered above him, breathing heavily and looking none too chipper himself. Glenn was about to take the poker away from him when Karl Webster arrived out of breath.

"Hey, Teddy. What'daya think you're doin'?" He quickly disarmed the elderly man and putting an arm around his shoulders guided him to Catkin's chair. Catkin jumped to the floor in time to avoid being sat upon, taking the bird missing from Irmajean's hat with him. He was swifter than her and as possession is said to be nine tenths of the law, the bird was still his.

"His blasted father is to blame." Ted gasped, gulped, and then continued in a rush as if his very existence depended on making a clean breast of everything. "It's his fault I couldn't ever join your mother. Couldn't ever be the kind of parent to you that I wanted to be. He says Walter stayed away from here. Well, he didn't. He came back when Clarice was married to Bertram. It seems Walter and Bertram were in cahoots to claim some of the money Walter felt was due him. Clarice idolized her brother and secretly kept in touch with him. They held a reunion on that ill-fated cruise where she met Bertram Willowby. Who, by the way, was introduced to her by

Walter. Walter came back to Pirate's Cove, although he
had to keep out of sight because of the bank theft. He
thought Bertram's secret society a hoot. Both men were
bigots. They scared Clarice's Chinese servant to death.
Threatened him with all sorts of unspeakable things. I
always liked Ling. Even though I was just a kid, he came
to me because they made him afraid for his life. I let him
hide in the attic and he died there of a heart attack. I didn't
know what to do and so I left him there. No one ever went
up into the attic..." Ted was trembling all over, gripping
the arms of the chair and looking like it might be the last
thing he ever did.

"Ted," Irmajean spoke in a reasonable tone of voice.
"How could something that happened when you were a
boy have kept you from joining your wife?"

"Mother didn't approve of my marriage. While I was
back East, she went upstairs in the attic for the first time I
could remember. She later told me she was looking for
suitcases so she could come visit me. Instead, she found
Ling. It was quite a shock—to both of us. She wired me to
come home—saying she'd found something in the attic
we needed to discuss. And, of course, she held that and
her subsequent ill health over my head."

"Ted, why didn't you just bury the body and have it out
of the way?"

Irmajean glanced at her husband as if to say that was
what she'd like to know.

Ted pulled a handkerchief from his pocket and wiped
his brow. "I couldn't bring myself to touch—him."

Given Ted's aversion to worms, slugs and the like,
Irmajean wasn't at all surprised. "Was the secret society

you knew existed the reason you and Barron claimed to be ignorant of the maze, the tunnel and the staircase?" Irmajean noticed with a lump in her throat that Ted clutched Karl Webster's hand as if that was the only thing holding him there.

"Our fathers had been a part of it, sucked in by slick talking Willowby. For a while he controlled the town, dictated who made it and who didn't. They were as glad as Clarice to see the back of him."

"Then why didn't they run him out of town earlier? Why did they leave it for her to do?"

"Because he knew too much about them by the time they caught on to the truth about him."

"What was finally the last straw with Clarice?"

"When she found out that they'd been terrorizing Ling. She thought—she never knew for certain what had happened to him. And after what did happen, I was afraid to tell anyone. Even Clarice."

Their question and answer session was punctuated by low groans from the floor where Frederick still lay sprawled.

The police were next to arrive; Chief Mallory shaking his head at the ill-assorted gathering in the library of Rosewood. Any fight that might have been left in Frederick was overridden by pain. As the police hauled him to his feet, he turned to Irmajean.

"Will you take care of Goblin for me? I don't want her to end up in a shelter. She's no trouble really." Then he added as if in final persuasion, "And she likes cats."

Stunned by his request, Irmajean said nothing. Instead, she sank down onto the recliner recently vacated by

Catkin. Many questions had been answered while some still hung fire. "Ted, what are you doing here? Not that we don't appreciate what you did, but physically you're not a match for Frederick. You could have been hurt or worse."

Karl threw back his head and laughed with delight. "I think, Mrs. Lloyd, that you're overlooking the obvious. Teddy was more than a match for Frederick. Never underestimate the element of surprise."

"Yes, well, I'll remember that. But really, what brought you here today?"

Again Karl answered for Ted. "I told Teddy that I'd shown you and Mr. Lloyd the body in his attic. He felt he had to explain and when you didn't answer your telephone, he supposed you were here. We arrived a few minutes before your confrontation with Freddy and the rest, as they say, is history."

Ted seemed at last goaded into summoning the energy for a response. "I couldn't let him get away with hurting anyone else. Not when I overheard you and found out who he was. The Carmichael men always got away with everything, and I wasn't about to let it continue. I'm tired," and there was a terrible weariness in his voice. "I no longer want to be a caretaker of the past or to pay for the mistakes of others."

"It's okay, Teddy. I'm here and I'll take care of you. Anybody that tries to get to you has to go through me first." And Karl gave Ted's shoulders a squeeze.

Neither Irmajean nor Glenn could help being moved by this honest display of affection. As quickly as the thought crossed Irmajean's mind that Karl Webster was a very forgiving man, she banished it. She would just be glad for

Ted's sake that he was. The past should be allowed to remain in the past. Especially as it had already wreaked too much havoc at Rosewood.

"Irmajean?"

"Yes, Ted, what is it?"

"I wasn't entirely honest with you and the police."

Well, that was no surprise, but she didn't say as much. "Oh, in what way?"

"I knew Priscilla had discovered the original plans to the property, but I was afraid to say so. She'd shown them to me and made a copy, which she stuck in the mail for you. I discovered that the other day and destroyed the copy. I'm sorry, and ordinarily I would never tamper with other people's mail, but I was afraid what might come out if Rosewood's secret places were found. You'd have known then the knowledge Barron and I and Chalmers, too, when he was alive, had been hiding all these years."

"Oh, Ted." If they'd told in the beginning what they knew about the maze, the tunnel and the staircase, Priscilla might still be alive. But then, the same could be said if Priscilla had left well enough alone. Stir up the past and bear the consequences. A secret wasn't a secret unless it was known by only one living person. Irmajean didn't remind Ted of the price tag attached to his and Barron's silence. She didn't have to. He knew only too well.

Epilogue

Irmajean sat in her comfortable rose-colored recliner and waited for the soap opera, *Dangerous Encounters*, to come on. When they'd left Rosewood the day before, Karl had stopped her with a half-whispered aside. "You mentioned once that Rose Campion didn't seem quite real, almost as if she was playing a part. Well, Rose and I go back a long way, and I have her permission to tell you to watch Channel 3 tomorrow at 2:30 pm."

Irmajean had to admit she was more than a little curious, even though she'd never been hooked on daytime TV. The opening of the show was definitely mood setting—car lights climbed up a twisting road that skirted a churning sea. Wind whipped the trees and the dark outline of a massive house waited at the end of the road. It was not hard to imagine a dangerous encounter awaiting the driver of the car.

Irmajean hadn't the faintest idea what was going on plot-wise and didn't care once it became apparent why Karl had suggested she watch this program. A gathering of bored and wealthy people stirred to attention when a human whirlwind entered the drawing room, colorful skirts flaring, bracelets flashing in the firelight and golden curls electric with vitality. A single line told it all, "The party can begin everyone! Rose Campion is here to tell you all what the future holds."

Irmajean gave a hoot of laughter, startling the huge black dog sprawled beside her chair. So she'd been right. The young woman they'd known as Rose Campion *had* been playing a part. No doubt her time in Pirate's Cove was understudy work for the role she played on TV. And no doubt her unexplained absences were accounted for by her need to be on the set. *Well, well. Now I know everything.* Or so Irmajean thought.

Meet Norma Seely

I live within sight of the Pacific Ocean with one husband, two dogs and two cats. I have a degree in history with a special interest in the unexplained. Writing has been a part of my life for almost forty years and I have nine published novels to my credit. Old houses, especially those with a mysterious past, have always intrigued me and inspired the background for *Maze Of Secrets*. Gardening, my heroine's passion, is a serious hobby of mine. The background for managing a historic property like the one in the story, comes from my oldest daughter (one of a set of twins) who was the assistant director for a house similar to the one in the story.